"What's wrong with your young man?"

Saul spoke with deceptive casualness, but Charlotte answered coldly, "Absolutely nothing."

"Well, the news of your wedding hit your father hard." He didn't need to remind her, and her angry resentment grew. "Why did you break it to him like that?" he asked.

"To show him I've made my own choice," she snapped back. "He seemed to think I might be in the running for you."

Saul echoed, "In the running?"

"As you've decided to settle down. As you're wife hunting. My father has this funny idea that I'm irresistible." She wanted him to sneer so she could fight back—tell him her opinion of him.

But he only said shortly, "That isn't his only mistake. The last thing I want is a wife!"

JANE DONNELLY
is also the author of these
Harlequin Romances

Diamond Cut Diamond

by

JANE DONNELLY

Harlequin Books

TORONTO • NEW YORK • LOS ANGELES • LONDON
AMSTERDAM • PARIS • SYDNEY • HAMBURG
STOCKHOLM • ATHENS • TOKYO • MILAN

Original hardcover edition published in 1982
by Mills & Boon Limited

ISBN 0-373-02510-6

Harlequin Romance first edition November 1982

CHAPTER ONE

THE girl galloped very fast across the field, crouched low over the horse's neck as though she was racing or being pursued. It had been a dry summer and the ground was hard. The pounding of her horse's hooves matched the throbbing in her head and she wasn't going back to the stables until she had worked some of the frustration out of her system. There was nothing like a good gallop to blow away the blues, and right now her mood was indigo.

Kelly, a magnificent four-year-old with gleaming chestnut flanks, was enjoying himself, going at full stretch, practically reinless, and Charlotte Dunscombe was a superb rider. They made a dashing pair, a handsome picture if there had been anyone watching. But the field was empty, and the first man to see them was not struck with admiration.

Kelly jumped a low hedge—he was good at hedges, he had been bred as a hunter—and Charlotte was giving him his head and the lane was a private road, there should have been no traffic on it. But at that moment a car rounded the bend and she reined frantically, causing Kelly to rear and whinney, while the car's brakes screamed as it took bumping evasive action over the grassy verge opposite.

Kelly was all right. He came down shuddering on four feet, but Charlotte's stomach dropped as sickeningly as though she had stepped down a lift shaft. She had had the fright of her life. She had had no idea that a car might be coming. The lane was only a track between two fields, both part of her father's small estate, and her mind had been on other things.

The driver and his car seemed undamaged. The car had drawn up, and the window had been wound down, and an angry-looking man was leaning out, shouting, 'What the hell do you think you're doing?'

'What are you? This is a private road. Can't you read?'

Normally she would have put that differently, but she had had a bad time in the past hour and if this trespasser wanted a row he had come to the right place. 'Roadhog!' she snarled. 'You must have been doing seventy round that bend!'

'Don't talk rubbish,' he snapped back, 'I was doing under thirty or I'd have hit you. Is the horse all right?'

Kelly was moving restlessly. He wanted to get galloping again. 'Seems to be,' she admitted. 'No thanks to you, though, you could have killed both of us!'

'If you're irresponsible enough to take the poor beast over hedges without making sure the road's clear,' he retorted, 'you shouldn't be in charge of a horse, somebody should be in charge of you!' and before she could come up with an answer to that he had driven away.

It *was* a private road, but it did connect one village with the next, and as they were about half way between the two there wouldn't be much point trying to catch him up and order him back. Besides, he didn't look the sort to take orders, so Charlotte trotted the horse along to the first gate and leaned over to open it.

Then she let Kelly break into a gallop again and went on with her therapy, only now she had a double cause of discontent. An extra bit of aggro to blow away. This was definitely not her day. She wasn't used to meeting men who scowled at her and couldn't get away from her fast enough.

Even angry men usually softened when they looked at Charlotte Dunscombe, because she was spectacularly beautiful, with long, long legs, smoky-blue eyes that tilted catlike, chestnut hair, perfect teeth and a translucent skin. She was twenty-one years old and could look about fourteen, and whatever she did men usually forgave her.

Not that she had ever done anybody much harm, she was basically a kind girl, but she had had her quota of scraping car paintwork—although this was the first time she had nearly landed a horse on top of a car—treading on toes in crowds and, of course, breaking dates and breaking off affairs that threatened to get too intense. Nearly always the men looked into the glowing oval of her face and said, 'There, there, that's all right,' or something along those lines.

The men who fell in love with her could be less understanding. None of them could claim that Charlotte had promised them anything, but they still left muttering about her not knowing what she did want, or being spoiled rotten, or having a father fixation.

The first time a boy blamed her father because she didn't respond to his advances she was sixteen, on holiday in Bournemouth with her father, and the boy, staying at the same hotel with his parents, was a sophisticated nineteen. He had a high opinion of himself and Charlotte was the prettiest girl in the hotel, he hadn't seen a prettier one in town, even if she didn't accept his opinions as holy writ. She had an annoying tendency to argue, usually preceding it with, 'My father says——' but she was alluringly sexy and apparently unaware of it.

They swam together and went to the seaside shows, and when he kissed her she was warm and sweet but amenable no further, and it was after a brief skirmish that took place when they were walking back in the moonlight to their hotel after a disco that he called her a 'daddy's girl'. 'God knows why,' he added spitefully, 'because your father's a pompous old fool.' He was a great believer in the generation gap, and that all fathers were fools, but he was taken completely by surprise by Charlotte's response.

She knocked him sprawling on the soft turf, not a shove either but a hard straight blow. Then she strode off, her lovely long legs covering the ground fast, and they never spoke to each other again.

Her father had roared with laughter when she told him, and she was laughing herself by then, because pompous and old were ridiculous applied to Colin Dunscombe. He was a marvellously understanding father, doting on her but letting her choose her own friends.

Charlotte had grown up in beauty. 'What an exquisite child,' was something she heard while she was still in her pram, and she had once gone into the kitchen and asked the housekeeper, 'What's a quizzit?' Miss Snowe had hidden a smile when she worked that one out, pronouncing, 'Handsome is as handsome does,' but privately agreeing with the description.

Charlotte had inherited her mother's looks. Her father was a handsome man, but her features and colouring were a replica of her mother's. The difference between them was that rheumatic fever had left the first Charlotte with a weak heart. When she was expecting her longed-for baby she was watched over tenderly by her husband, care and money were lavished on her, and the baby was born, a perfect little girl, and Colin Dunscombe thanked God that he had both his wife and his daughter.

But before baby Charlotte's first birthday her mother went down with a 'flu virus that was plaguing the country but only striking in deadly fashion at the weak and the old. All her husband's money couldn't save her. Charlotte had no memories of her mother, only the stories that other people told her, but her home had always been filled with love.

Inevitably she had measured the men who came along against her father, and at twenty-one she still had plenty of time for looking. Only now she was in love.

Reaching the top of a hill, she jumped down from the horse and tethered his bridle to a tree. The hot sun shone on them and after a moment the horse began to crop in the shade while Charlotte flung herself down on the grass. A little breeze reached them up here and she pulled off the cap she was wearing and her thick waving chestnut hair cascaded over her shoulders. It was glorious hair. If there was a girl who had everything it was probably Charlotte Dunscombe, and she knew how lucky she was, especially since she had found Jeremy.

She would be meeting him in an hour or so, and she felt quite faint with longing, a rush of heat to the head and heart. This had to be love, and it was a very exciting sensation. Thinking about Jeremy was the next best thing to being with him. It was making her feel better already.

Their lunch together wouldn't be the celebration she'd hoped, but maybe it wasn't too bad. Nothing was final, nothing couldn't be changed. She wouldn't believe that she couldn't get her own way in the end.

She rode back at a staider pace, trotting along the track between the hawthorn hedges. Birds were singing and the hum of bees filled the air. The cabbage white butterflies fluttered over a bank of wild thyme, and when she turned into the courtyard at the back of the house two golden retrievers came bounding to meet her.

She fussed them for a moment, then rubbed Kelly down and slipped a blanket over him, and left him in his stable. She loved this house. She loved Tria and Wilbur the dogs, she loved Kelly. She dearly loved the immensely fat woman who was chopping chives in the kitchen, and who answered to 'Aunt Lucy', although Miss Snowe was no blood relation. She had been housekeeper here when the first Charlotte arrived as a bride. It was her hand that the dying girl had clutched to whisper, 'Look after my baby.'

Nobody knew that, but Lucy Snowe, and God knows Mr
Colin cared for his daughter more than he cared for himself, but to Lucy Snowe, spinster, Charlotte was her own
dear child.

Now she looked up from her task as Charlotte walked
in and asked, 'Meeting your latest?'

'You know I am.' Charlotte had told her yesterday that
she was lunching with Jeremy today and asked if she
wanted any shopping done in town. Charlotte had always
had boy-friends and Aunt Lucy must guess that this time
was different, but she still insisted on acting as though all
Jeremy was was another friend.

That bothered Charlotte a little. She had been disappointed when she introduced him and Aunt Lucy went
on bustling around, because he was so special that she
had expected her to be impressed. Women drooled over
Jeremy. They came up and asked for his autograph now
and within a year or so he was going to be famous. When
she apologised Jeremy said of course it didn't matter. He
hadn't expected her to recognise him. The old duck looked
a bit past active theatregoing and his TV appearances
had been brief.

But Charlotte would have liked to talk to her about
Jeremy. It had been Aunt Lucy's wide lap she had
climbed on to as a child, to hear stories and to tell secrets.
Her father always tried to find time for her, but he was a
busy man. Aunt Lucy was around all the time, and
Charlotte told her almost everything. Secrets were safe
with her. Charlotte might have confided that she had
fallen in love, given a little encouragement, but Aunt
Lucy's famous perception didn't seem to be working over
Jeremy.

'You'll be in for dinner, won't you?' said Aunt Lucy
now. 'Your father's expecting you here.'

'I know,' said Charlotte, biting her lip.

'And what's wrong with that?' She hadn't missed the shadow on Charlotte's face, and Charlotte almost admitted, 'We've just had a fearful row. The first ever. It might be better if we kept out of each other's way for the rest of the day.' But that would horrify Aunt Lucy, and now that a little time had elapsed Charlotte could hardly believe it herself. By evening surely things would be all right again.

'Nothing's wrong,' she said. 'I'll be home in time.'

The two dogs had stayed dozing on the flagstones outside, and now Charlotte stuck her head round the door of the drawing room where a tiny pale-caramel-coloured pekingese flicked its tail in welcome. 'It's all right, Georgy,' she said, 'it's me.'

Georgy would have won a prize for prettiness, with his black velvet mask and long silky hair, but although he had a faultless pedigree and pekes are famed for courage— the lion-dogs of Imperial China—this peke was an arrant coward. It took very little to have Georgy scuttling for shelter, but in between panics he was comic and loving, and in Charlotte he saw his protector against a world that was out to get him.

When Charlotte was around he walked with head up and sweeping tail held high, and now he followed her upstairs and lay on the rug at the foot of her bed while she changed her shoes for pink flat-heeled pumps that matched her pink cotton shirt. She was wearing jeans and she twisted a pink scarf bandeau-fashion to hold back her hair from her face. Single diamond earrings sparkled in her ears and the ice-blue of an oval aquamarine in a plain gold setting was very effective against the smooth tan of her hand.

She opened a jewellery box that stood on the dressing table and stood for a moment thoughtfully considering the contents. Most women would have considered this a fantastic collection: rings, earrings, bracelets, a tangle of gold chains, and Charlotte had more valuable jewellery still in the house safe and the bank; but she didn't look as though the sight of it was giving her any pleasure. She sighed deeply, closing the lid, and turned to scoop up Georgy. He could manage getting up the stairs, but going down sometimes proved too much for him and he closed his eyes and lost his footing.

The two retrievers looked up hopefully as she opened the garage doors, but when she said, 'No,' they went back to their drowsing. She often took them with her, but it would be too hot to leave the three of them in the car while she had lunch and it was no fun walking a pack through the busy streets. She dropped Georgy on the passenger seat and drove her scarlet sports car through the gates of the small elegant Georgian house that looked out across the green to the church and churchyard.

It took her a little under half an hour to reach town and she made for where she knew she would find a parking space, at the back of Dunscombe's impressive salons. This was the family firm, her father was the third generation and a respected name in the jewellery business. Inside the shop were dark blue velvet walls and a mirrored ceiling, and cases of precious gems in gold, silver and platinum. In the courtyard behind were the offices and workrooms where jewellery was designed and made.

Charlotte parked her car alongside the row of staff cars, climbed out with Georgy under her arm and called a cheery, 'Hi,' to a young man and a girl who were chatting together at the top of a flight of steps leading to the office floor.

They both answered her, but as she walked out of the yard the girl muttered, 'It's not fair, is it, all she's got? I bet she doesn't do much clocking in at nine in the mornings!'

The girl was a salesgirl from a gift shop, and she would have envied Charlotte even if Charlotte had been flat broke, because Charlotte looked like a top model and she didn't. 'And,' she added bitchily, 'it wouldn't surprise me if that hair's a wig!'

Charlotte had a natural flair for jewellery design. She would have been happy working here, but it had always been impressed on her that she was needed as her father's hostess first and foremost. And she modelled their products. She enjoyed dressing up in striking fashions and wearing the complimentary accessories, but she looked just as eye-catching, in casual clothes, as she threaded her way along the crowded pavements of the old Cotswold town.

The sun was shining and the pubs and restaurants seemed to be crowded, mostly with tourists. A crowd of young folk who looked like students were eating sandwiches and drinking Cokes, sitting on the steps of the crumbling Anglo-Saxon cross in the middle of the town square, and Charlotte wondered why they didn't go down to the river because it was hot up here and dusty.

The idea of a picnic by the river was appealing. When she met Jeremy for lunch they usually ate at the Stage Door, which was the pub nearest the theatre, but on a sultry day like this the little garden at the back would be full, and she went into the bakers and came out with wrapped sandwiches and apple pies in a carrier bag, then into the shop next door for fruit and two cans of lager.

The Little Theatre had stood in the middle of Chipping Queanton since Victorian times. Their main repertoire was Shakespeare and the classics, but each season they put on some experimental work by living playwrights.

Charlotte was still fifteen minutes early for her lunch date, so she looked at the posters outside, although she knew them by heart. 'This week—*Quality Street*, by J. M.

Barrie,' and the cast list with Jeremy Wylde's name nearly at the top. Inside the glass-fronted cases were photographs taken from the play and there was Jeremy of course, looking terrific. She had copies of all these at home, he had presented her with them, but she stood looking, dreaming herself into the picture until Georgy gave a yelp at her ankles and she realised that a dear old lady was about to pat him.

Then she picked him up and walked into the foyer, had a few words with the girl in the booking kiosk, and went into the theatre to sit at the back of the stalls and watch the final minutes of this morning's rehearsal.

She couldn't take her eyes off Jeremy. He seemed to her far and away the best actor of them all, dominating the scene, although that might have been because she had arrived when he was the one doing the talking. All the rest had to do right now was listen as Jeremy went into a tirade about corruption in high places.

This was one of the new plays, and though Jeremy's voice was ringing with sincerity and three other members of the cast were in attitudes of rapt attention Charlotte had doubts whether it would grab the audience. She had read the script and it hadn't grabbed her, but with all her heart she wished it success.

Her first sight of Jeremy Wylde had been in this theatre. She had gone along with a girl friend to see Shaw's *The Devil's Disciple* and Jeremy was the new actor who had recently joined the company from a repertory up north.

As the dashing Dick Dudgeon, she had thought, 'Wow, I could have a crush on him!' and laughed at herself because this was all part of the fun. It wasn't real any more than the play was. But when she went backstage and met him the glamour was still there. The man close to, in the flesh, was exactly like the character he had played. He had stripped off his make-up, but the skin underneath was tanned and, as he lounged in a chair in front of his dressing table in the room he shared with two other actors, the stage manager let Charlotte and her friend in. 'Two young local ladies,' he'd announced, 'come to tell you what they thought of your performance.'

Jeremy had turned with languid charm, cynical and a shade weary, but when he saw Charlotte his heavy-lidded eyes opened wide. She was wearing a shirt and skirt covered with scarlet poppies on white, her hair seemed copper-coloured in the electric light, and the general effect was stunning. This was no ordinary local girl. This one, he would have sworn, had ambitions to get on the stage herself. 'You've got to be an actress,' he said, and when she shook her head, smiling, 'A model, then.'

'Only for the family firm.'

'And they own *Vogue* magazine.'

She laughed, 'No such luck. We just make a few rings and things.'

Next day was Sunday and he came for her after lunch, impressed as much by the house as he was by the girl, noticing the marks of affluence and putting himself out to charm.

There was a drizzle of rain as they walked around the almost deserted gardens of a National Trust stately house, treading velvet lawns, sitting on the wall of a pond covered with flat lily leaves under which golden fish darted and flashed, while Jeremy told Charlotte the story of his life.

She was enthralled. She went with him through drama school, with a travelling theatre group, Preston Rep, and now the Little Theatre. Chipping Queanten was on the way to Stratford-on-Avon and she had no doubts, and neither did he, that he was destined for the heights.

Neither bothered about the rain. It curled the tendrils of Charlotte's hair and put a pearly mist on her skin, and although he lived and worked among beautiful women

Jeremy Wylde thought he had rarely seen a lovelier one. They were sitting in a little stone folly that was open to the weather, and he suddenly got up and jumped down the three entrance steps to appear just beneath the window through which she was watching him, straight into the balcony scene from *Romeo and Juliet*.

'But, soft! what light through yonder window breaks? It is the east and Juliet is the sun!'

She almost giggled, but he was giving it a serious rendering in his beautiful actor's voice, and there was no one else in sight, and as she looked down into the handsome face she began to thrill to the magic of the words. At the end of the speech she took her cue and sighed 'Ah me.'

'She speaks——' He was transported with delight and they played out a little more of the scene, all alone, until Charlotte ran out of words and sighed again, 'Ah me!' and spread her hands wide with a rueful expression. Then he came back into the folly and took her in his arms and said, 'I know now why Romeo was ready to die for Juliet.'

Later she thought that she had fallen in love then. That was less than three months ago, but it seemed to Charlotte that she had known Jeremy for ever. Or perhaps it was because she had always been waiting for someone like him.

He spotted her now and jumped down from the stage, and she stood up, lifting Georgy from her lap into her arms. Jeremy kissed her cheek while Georgy grizzled. 'Been here long?' he asked.

'Not long.'

'How was I?'

'Fabulous.'

He gave a modest grin but would have been irritated by any other verdict. 'And how did it go with you?' He had known the answer to his first question, but this one he asked with some anxiety, and Charlotte sighed,

'Not so good.'

'But I thought——'

'I got some sandwiches,' she said. 'Shall we eat them by the river? Everywhere seems to be full.'

'If you like, but what exactly——'

'I'll tell you all about it.' She didn't want to talk where the others could hear. Jeremy had assured her he wouldn't mention it to anyone, but she couldn't be sure, and if he had it was going to be a disappointment to them too.

He hurried her through the crowds, taking the carrier bag in one hand and her arm in the other. She understood his concern, and when they reached the towpath she let him choose the first empty spot on the river bank to dump the carrier bag and have their picnic.

'Well?' he asked, 'what did he say?' Charlotte opened the bag keeping Georgy tethered to her with the loop of the leash over her wrist, although Georgy (not one to wander) had already collapsed beside her.

'He said no,' she said, and Jeremy smote himself on the forehead with the flat of his hand and swore. She knew it was a struggle for him to go on in a calm reasoning way, because what he wanted to do was go on cursing. But he said quietly,

'I know I don't seem to hit it off too well with him, but did you explain that this is purely a business proposition?'

'I tried to.' She pulled back the tags on the lager cans and one foamed out all over her hands. She was puzzled still. 'I really don't understand it myself.' She opened the sandwich packs and Jeremy shook his head, and she began to pull a sandwich apart, tossing the pieces to the ducks and swans that came zooming in from all along the river bank.

This morning she had knocked on her father's study door. Usually she chose evenings to catch him in a good mood. She had had plenty of experience in cajolement, she had been wrapping him round her little finger all her life, but he had been out for the last two nights and this evening they had guests for dinner. She'd thought she'd ask over breakfast. But he skipped breakfast and took coffee and the mail into his study, and after giving him a few minutes to open the letters she followed.

His, 'Come in,' sounded preoccupied. Charlotte always tapped, but she always opened the door because she knew he would never want to keep her out, and he smiled as soon as he saw her.

'I want to talk to you,' she'd said. 'Please.'

He looked down at his mail as she took a chair and placed it facing him, and sat with her chin in her hands, elbows on the desk. This pose was a small joke between them. When she was a child she had often sat like that, chin cupped, when she was thoughtful, and her father had said, 'There's my little sobersides.' Now he said, 'A real heart-to-heart, is it?'

'In a way I suppose so. I want to make an investment.'

'You do?' She never had before. The only business she knew anything about was their own, and that had been enough for her. Her father waited and she went on, 'The Little Theatre is having a hard time staying solvent. They need a patron.'

His face hardened slightly. 'My dear, we're not living in the eighteenth century,' he said. So it wasn't going to be that easy.

'All right,' she made a funny face, 'that's an old-fashioned word, but I do want us to put some money into it.'

'And this is Jeremy Wylde's idea?'

'In a way, I suppose. Not entirely.' Everybody around here knew that the theatre played to good houses while there were holidaymakers, but not many tourists came in

the winter and there weren't enough theatre-loving locals
to fill it week after week. Inflation was sending expenses
sky high and the box office receipts couldn't cover them.

An appeal had been launched, 'Friends of the Little
Theatre', but it hadn't brought in enough, and last week
while they were discussing this Jeremy had said suddenly,
'Your father's loaded, isn't he?'

It was during the afternoon. Jeremy had driven over to
Charlotte's home where she was working on pendant designs, sitting at the little davenport desk in the drawing
room. 'We get by,' she'd said.

'How about asking him if he'd consider bailing us out?'

She had been doubtful at first. Her father, who had
always welcomed her friends, had been inexplicably dist-
ant with Jeremy. Although when Charlotte challenged
him he had insisted she was mistaken.

But the Little Theatre was a good cause and the more
she thought about it the more eager she was to help. Her
father was signing a cheque for twenty-five pounds now
and she said, 'It's a start, but it's thousands they need.'

'Not from us,' he said.

He bought paintings, pieces of sculpture. Not recently,
but she could remember him spending what seemed to be
vast sums, and acting was an art form. Our culture was
poorer with every theatre that closed. She said, 'I suppose
it is a lot to ask, but——' But he had never denied her
anything before: clothes, cars, holidays, a more than
generous allowance.

'*No!*' He shook his head as he spoke.

She had hardly any hard cash, but of course she did
have some beautiful things, and even if her father stayed
adamant there was no reason why she shouldn't do her
own investing. She asked, 'Well, can I sell something?'

'Sell what?'

'Some of my jewellery, maybe.'

'I wouldn't hear of it.'

Even when she was a child he had never laid down the law. He had always explained his orders and they had always been reasonable and fair. He had to be carrying on like this because he had taken this dislike to Jeremy, and that was so out of character, because he had always been affable to her boy-friends. Several had wanted to marry her and he had always said the choice was hers, he would be happy if she was happy. Now she asked him bluntly, 'Do you know anything about Jeremy that I don't know?'

'No.' He looked straight at her, and she believed him.

'But you don't like him?'

'I don't dislike him, although I found him rather a boring young man.'

'*Boring?* Jeremy? You're *joking!*'

He wasn't joking, and she stopped smiling and said quietly, 'But it's mine, my jewellery, I can do what I like with it.'

'In the legal sense very little is yours,' he said.

The fabulous pieces were family heirlooms, she wouldn't have been selling them anyway, and it hurt her to be reminded that the stones her mother had worn, and that she wore now, did not belong to her. She said bitterly, 'I suppose I own my last birthday present?'

That was the aquamarine ring. The diamond ear-studs had been a Christmas gift, and her father said heavily, 'I can't stop you selling your trinkets and giving the money to anyone you choose. But it would displease me, I'd be very reluctant to replace them. In fact if you did that, I'd take steps to see that you got your hands on nothing of real value while I'm alive.'

Charlotte had never seen him like this before in all her life. Skin mottled and mouth grim with anger. 'While I'm alive,' he had said. That meant, 'Until I'm dead,' and she realised how much grey there was in the thick light-brown hair. She hadn't noticed that before. He had been fifteen years older than her mother, but with his tall slim figure and almost unlined face he had always seemed a young father. Now she saw his hands shaking and she thought incredulously, 'He's growing *old*!'

That frightened her, throwing her into confusion. Losing her temper was easier than facing up to that, and she blazed, 'That's a pretty high-handed attitude to take! You think it's a con-trick, do you, the Little Theatre? It's been there for nearly seventy years, but you still think it's a fly-by-night? Or is it just Jeremy you don't trust?'

'Put it this way,' said her father. 'I do not feel inclined to invest beyond this amount,' he tapped the cheque for twenty-five pounds still lying on his desk, 'in that young man's future.'

'What if I do?' Her indignation made her eloquent. 'You say you know nothing about him that I don't know, so your attitude has to be sheer prejudice. I'd never have expected you to make decisions when you've no facts to go on. Intuition, just on its own, can be pretty unreliable, you know, unless you're using a crystal ball.'

'I grant you that,' said her father. 'But why should your intuition be sounder than mine? I do have years of experience behind me.' He turned back to the letter she had been reading when she came in and told her, 'Tell your friend that you're in no position to sponsor anybody and I'm not in the market.'

She didn't tell Jeremy this word for word. She tried to make it less personal, but the verdict was the same. Dunscombes were not coming to the rescue of the Little Theatre.

She felt now that she had let Jeremy down and she was disappointed on her own account. It would have been fun, getting involved with the theatre, but if she helped

her father was going to take it badly. For no reason at all
he did not like Jeremy.

'You know what I think?' said Jeremy, skimming a
piece of apple across the water into the flapping melee of
ducks. 'I think your old man's jealous of me.'

'Oh *no*!' But she couldn't help wondering, because
Jeremy was the only man, besides her father, who had
really mattered to her. She hadn't told them that at home,
but perhaps her manner had shown it and perhaps her
father was resenting second place. All the same she shook
her head emphatically. 'You don't know him. That
wouldn't be like him.'

But this morning hadn't been like him either. She had
hardly recognised the flushed, angry man, and she turned
the ring on her finger and said with a wry little laugh as
though it was a joke, 'Although he did threaten to dis-
inherit me if I sold any of my stuff and put the proceeds
into the theatre.'

'You're kidding!' Jeremy was shocked. 'He couldn't do
that. Could he?'

'He didn't actually put it that strongly.' She wished she
hadn't mentioned it now.

'But he's going to take some getting round?'

'If you're planning staying around me,' she said. 'Yes.'

'Oh, I am.' He leaned across and kissed her, and then
smiled at a couple of women who had recognised him
from last night's play and were watching with interest.
He could charm anybody, Charlotte thought. My father's
going to like him before long, because I hope he'll be
around for the rest of my life.

They ate their picnic, with no further reference to
financial crises, and by the time she was packing up the
leftovers she was feeling happier than she had all day. It
was a bore that she had to be home for dinner tonight.
She would have liked to meet Jeremy after the evening

performance, and have supper with him. But that was out of the question because they were expecting old friends, and a business colleague, and when Jeremy asked, 'No chance of you getting away for an hour or two tonight?' she had to say 'No chance at all, but I'll try for lunch tomorrow.'

'Sure.' She was getting into her car and he leaned through the window to kiss her again and said suddenly, 'Don't do anything rash, sweetheart. No sense riling your father.'

That was considerate, and sensible because she was sure they would win him round eventually, and tonight, some time, she would say sorry for losing her temper this morning. If her father didn't want to invest in the theatre he was entitled to refuse. It was so much more important that he should put aside his prejudices against Jeremy. That was what she had to work on.

She thought about it on the way home. She would have to arrange a few more casual meetings. They hadn't really had a chance to get to know each other yet. When they did of course her father would like him. Life had always been good to Charlotte, but love really was a many-splendoured thing and it was unthinkable that anything should mar the happiness she and Jeremy were finding together.

She spent what was left of the afternoon in the garden. It was mostly lawns now, because the gardening staff had dwindled over the years and was now down to old Tom and he had lumbago. Charlotte liked gardening. She had green fingers and the strength to handle lawnmowers and hedgecutters. She weeded for a while, then came back into the house to change into a bikini and collect sun oil, towel and a novel, and sunbathed for an hour or so.

The patio with its circular arbour was out of sight of the main building. Bright flowers filled old stone troughs and a purple wisteria and red honeysuckle rambled over the trellises. In one corner of the flagstones was a bigger-than-lifesize carving of a hound, commissioned by one of Charlotte's ancestors, and beside him a cheap modern garden ornament in roughcast of a peke.

Charlotte had bought that herself, off a market stall when she was seven years old and had an earlier peke, one of the fearless kind, as her pet. She had placed it proudly in the drawing room, on the smooth surface of an exquisite Regency table, and been bewildered when Aunt Lucy screeched and grabbed it, then went down on her knees to start examining the table for scratches.

It had been explained to Charlotte that this, like the hound, who had probably been lonely for a long time, was an outdoor dog; and fourteen years later he was still here, his bright brown-glass marble eyes still staring.

Georgy was in the shadow of the arbour, flat, with feet outstretched, his stomach getting the cool benefit of the stone floor, while Charlotte lay, gleaming gold, soaking up the sunshine. She rolled over after a while, unhooking her bra, and the heat was pleasantly soothing on her shoulder blades so that she drowsed off and woke yawning.

It was time to go in. Georgy was snoring his small head off, and she rehooked her bra and got up reluctantly. She liked the couple who were eating with them tonight, but they were her father's friends and generation and rather an earnest pair. It wouldn't be much fun, and if she hadn't had that scene this morning she might have asked her father to make some excuse for her.

As it was she had better be there. And better get herself dressed. This was hardly suitable get-up for entertaining the Rural Dean and his wife.

She walked into the house through the long drawing-room windows that opened into the garden, and as she did the phone on a side table rang. She picked it up and a moment later Aunt Lucy opened the hall door to hear Charlotte say, 'Oh, I am sorry, Mrs Reynolds.' The Reynolds were the couple they had been expecting to dinner. Aunt Lucy sighed and stayed. 'What wretched luck,' said Charlotte, 'it must be terribly painful. Perhaps next week?'

When she put down the phone Aunt Lucy asked,

'Not coming?'

'He's turned his ankle,' said Charlotte, 'and it's puffing up like a balloon. I wonder if this lets me off the hook. I mean, there's only some old business codger, surely my father can chat him up himself.'

Georgy let out a yelp and began to back, crablike, from a winged armchair at the other end of the room. A man got up, Georgy went on yelping, and Charlotte recognised the face that had glared at her through the window when Kelly had nearly landed on his car.

He was tall, with dark hair, dark eyebrows, and shock made her temporarily speechless. He said, 'Miss Dunscombe, I presume?'

'Yes. You're——?'

'The old business codger.' His smile was everything a smile should be, showing excellent teeth, but her tongue was sticking to the roof of her mouth and her speech was jerky.

'I'm sorry about that. But then I was only guessing, and you are rather early for dinner at eight, and if you'd stood up a little sooner——' The towel, draped around her shoulders, slithered as she moved, and as she jerked to grab it the hook she hadn't quite slipped into place on her bra gave, and her bra slid off, leaving her topless. It was like a scene from a *Carry On* movie. 'Hell's bells!' she muttered, clutching everything she could around her as she got out of the room.

In the hall Georgy barked furiously at the closed door and Aunt Lucy stood trying to look shocked. 'I'm thankful the Reverend wasn't here,' said Aunt Lucy.

Charlotte grinned. 'It's all this oil all over me—I'm slippery as an eel. Good job the bottom half was secure. I'd better get into a bath.'

'You better had,' agreed Aunt Lucy.

When she reached her bedroom Charlotte went to the window. The sun was setting and there were clouds in the sky and the perspiration on the palms of her hands was cold. She had mocked at intuition this morning. 'Unless you're using a crystal ball,' she had said, with all the sarcasm she could muster. But this uneasy feeling now, warning her against the man downstairs, was like second sight. There had been an aura of menace about him. And what was a stranger doing, sitting all alone in the drawing room as though he had known them all his life, or as though this was his own home?

CHAPTER TWO

CHARLOTTE dressed for dinner in a strange state of mind. It was unusual for her to feel apprehensive about meeting anyone, but she had made an idiot of herself twice today with this man, and she blushed at the memory.

She wished she could laugh about it. The first time, with Kelly, had been a bit of criminal negligence, but just now was funny in a way. She wasn't one of the topless brigade, but she had wandered among them unembarrassed on the beaches of St Tropez, wearing a strip of bra that hardly counted, and anyway her breasts were young and firm. She tried to tell herself what had happened had been comic, but she would have given a lot to have clipped that clasp into place and avoided the whole incident.

Her next appearance had better be circumspect, and she chose a plain white dress, sleeveless with thin shoulder straps, and wore it with a round gold slave bangle on her upper arm, and gold sandals. She brushed her hair until it shone, swept it sideways so that only one ear was revealed and wore a single gold pearl-shaped dropper earring.

She wished she was dressing for Jeremy. It would have been lovely if he had been the one downstairs tonight, waiting for her, given the run of the house by her father like this stranger. She dabbed perfume on pulse spots and went to the window again and looked out across the gardens. It was a heavy night, very still, the few clouds seemed motionless and she thought, I wouldn't be surprised if we get thunder. She had a feeling that something

was about to break around her and it was probably a
storm.

'What's he doing downstairs all on his own?' she said
aloud, addressing Georgy as he was the only one there.
He lifted his ears and put his head on one side and
appeared to consider the question, and Charlotte said,
'Let's go and ask somebody, shall we?'

Most days Aunt Lucy had help around the house from
Maudie, a young married woman who went home to her
family. Aunt Lucy lived here, of course. This had been
her home for the last forty years and while the
Dunscombes stayed so would she. She was in the kitchen
now, preparing the herb sauce for the rainbow trout, and
as Charlotte donned a long bibbed apron she said,
'Shouldn't you be joining the company?'

Charlotte shrugged. Her father liked her around when
they entertained, but tonight she was less than enthusi-
astic. She asked, 'Who *is* he?'

'Name of Laurenson.' Aunt Lucy added a pinch more
tarragon.

'And?' Charlotte prompted.

'That's all I know. Your father says "This is Mr
Laurenson".'

'Well, he seems to be making himself at home.' She
was resentful, although they had something of an open
house here. Both she and her father had a wide social
circle. Only her father didn't seem to be welcoming
Jeremy and she would have preferred Mr Laurenson to
have stayed away.

Aunt Lucy tested the sauce again before she enquired,
'Why? What was he doing?'

'Just sitting, I suppose,' Charlotte had to admit, adding,
'And jumping out of the shadows. I felt a right fool, I can
tell you.' Again hot colour flared in her cheeks and Aunt
Lucy said philosophically,

'I expect he's seen a naked woman before.'

'I *wasn't* naked!' It was ages since she could remember blushing, but now it seemed she couldn't stop.

'In my day,' mused Aunt Lucy, 'if a girl had carried on like that she'd never have shown her face again. But we wore real foundations, not bits of ribbon. Measured for them, we were.'

Aunt Lucy was still measured, her corsets were little miracles of engineering, and Charlotte stifled a giggle. By no stretch of imagination could she visualise Aunt Lucy's bra slipping off. 'I suppose I'd better go,' she said.

The starters, melon, grapefruit and grape cocktails, looked cool and pretty, and the trout was local, served with the herb sauce and cucumber. Then there was Aunt Lucy's special treacle tart and cream, and cheese, of course. It would be a good meal. It always was. Her father ought to be satisfied with his womenfolk and his home at the end of that, and Charlotte wondered if there was hope of a word alone with him before they all sat down. She would have liked to put things right. But if she got no chance to apologise she would have to settle for actions speaking louder than words, and being very conciliatory and as nice as pie over dinner.

Perhaps she would invite Jeremy round for a meal on Sunday. Facing him over a table her father would have to talk and listen, and Jeremy was anxious to please and it was an idea. She said suddenly, 'Aunt Lucy, what do you think of Jeremy?'

'A nice enough young man, I'm sure,' said Aunt Lucy, noncommittally.

'I think he's more than that,' said Charlotte.

'Then he probably is.' Aunt Lucy wasn't arguing.

'But my father doesn't like him, and I want them to get on, so what do you think I ought to do?' Aunt Lucy's advice had always been sound and this was a real problem, but all she said was,

'I think you ought to get in there and show Mr
Laurenson what you look like with your clothes on.' She
wasn't taking Jeremy seriously, nor Charlotte, and
Charlotte wondered if she still thought of her as a child.

She said quietly, 'Aunt Lucy, I am twenty-one.'

'I know.' Aunt Lucy decanted the sauce from pan to
tureen. 'And I'm sixty-one—what are we talking about?'

'Nothing,' said Charlotte.

She went looking for her father and Mr Laurenson.
The drawing room was empty. She walked down the
length of it because the men might be strolling on the
lawns, but the garden, seen from the windows, seemed
deserted. Nothing had changed in this room since
Charlotte was born, not even the carpets. Everything had
a serene air of ageless elegance, but tonight she felt disturbed, disorientated.

It had been an upsetting day. Especially this morning's
scene with her father. She had thought he might say yes,
because he was a generous man who did support good
causes. At any rate she'd hoped for a sizeable contribution
to the theatre's funds from him. She had never thought
he would threaten her. That they would end up *quarrel-
ling*.

She wished the Reynolds had been coming tonight with
their friendly familiar faces, saving her from an evening
almost alone with a stranger. With Georgy trotting at her
heels she went into the small parlour, then looked into the
dining room, and finally tapped on the study door and
walked in there.

The man sitting in her father's chair behind her father's
desk was Laurenson, and Georgy, who had ambled
happily into the room, took one look at him and darted
out between Charlotte's feet, sending her off balance. It
was a wonder she didn't go flat on her face. As it was she

lurched forward and grabbed the desk edge like a drunk needing support—a very undignified entry. It seemed she couldn't get near this man without doing something ridiculous.

'Where's my father?' she gasped.

He looked at his watch. 'On his way home, I should think. He had to go back to the office.'

Leaving this man behind and without mentioning it to Charlotte. But he surely hadn't invited Mr Laurenson to sit down at his desk and go through his papers, and she said, 'Do you mind? Some of this is rather confidential.'

He smiled at her. He had a curving sensuous mouth. 'Not this file, I think you'll find.' He closed the blue cardboard folder and stood up, and of course he was remembering her strip-tease, and she wondered whether she should try to make a joke of it. But she couldn't have been funny to save her life. All she could get out was, 'If you've quite finished!' sounding snappish.

'For now,' he said, and Charlotte couldn't bring herself to ask what that meant. She led the way towards the drawing room while Georgy yelped incessantly at the bottom of the stairs. 'If you'll excuse me, I'll put him somewhere safe,' she said. 'Where he can't see you.'

'Where he can't see me?' One dark brow quirked, and she carried Georgy to Aunt Lucy in the kitchen. 'Keep him here, will you? He's being a nuisance as usual,' and she hurried back into the hall to explain, 'He's scared of strangers. And it's not that he's ever been ill-treated, it's just that he was born with this over-developed sense of self-preservation.'

'Very sensible in this day and age,' said Laurenson, who obviously thought this was the kind of daft dog she would have. He had walked into the drawing room and stood facing her, but it took quite an effort for her to face him.

'Do you think it's best to run?' she asked.

'That depends on the opposition.'

'Yes, it would. Do sit down. Do have a drink.' She had played hostess in this house as long as she could remember, but she had never felt or sounded as gauche as this before. Something about him drained her confidence away. Perhaps the fact that his eyes were so dark and piercing, as though they looked right through her and nothing about her could ever surprise him.

'Mr Laurenson, isn't it?' she said.

'Saul Laurenson.'

'I'm Charlotte Dunscombe.' Which he knew, of course, and on which he made no comment. He was sitting now, and very much at ease from his stance, very relaxed.

'Whisky?' she suggested.

'Thank you.'

She went to a side table and picked up the Georgian decanter and her hands were shaking so that she spilt the drink, although the tumbler top was surely wide enough. She rolled her eyes ceilingwards in exasperation. He gave her the jitters, sitting there contributing nothing, and it wasn't as though he was bashful or overwhelmed by her looks as more than one man had been. On the contrary.

She gave him his drink and sat down herself, then for what seemed an age she could think of nothing to say worth saying. There was always the weather—'Isn't it lovely? Aren't we having a super summer after that wet spring?' But that sounded as banal as everything else that came into her head, although she wouldn't have thought there was a man alive who could have reduced her to this strangling shyness.

At last she asked, 'Are you in our line of business?'

'In a way,' he said, and nothing more, and Charlotte thought, He's enjoying stretching out the silences. And then, No, he isn't, he's simply bored. He doesn't think I'm worth talking to, he thinks I'm a dumb-bell.

She was used to men going more than half way to meet her, although she had coaxed retiring folk out of their shells before. She swallowed. 'Are you going to be around here for long?'

'Possibly.' He didn't sound particularly brusque, although he could hardly have been more laconic.

'That's nice,' she said, and thought, Not here, I hope. Not where you and I are likely to meet. 'Where do you come from?' she asked, and he said, 'The Blue Boar.'

That was a local hotel, he was making a fool of her, and she wanted to say, 'Look, I didn't invite you. It's giving me no pleasure sitting here trying to entertain you. And as you'd obviously rather be alone, goodnight to you.'

What she did say was, 'Would you excuse me, I want to have a word with Lucy?'

It would be just before the curtain was due to go up in the theatre, and she rang Jeremy. 'It's Charlotte.'

'Anything wrong?' He presumed it had to be an emergency, and it was in a small way, although she tried to laugh.

'I just need a confidence booster. There's the most frightful man here, my father's asked him to dinner, and he makes my tongue stick to the roof of my mouth. Everything I do goes wrong. He seems to be paralysing my central nervous system. There are folk like that, aren't there? A sort of Dracula without the fangs.'

Jeremy laughed. 'You can't win 'em all.'

'I don't want to win him!' she shrieked. 'I just want to talk to somebody who thinks I'm O.K. He thinks I'm a cretin.'

'You're beautiful and I love you,' said Jeremy.

'Thank you, thank you.' She was smiling now. This

had really just been an excuse to talk to Jeremy, because he was beautiful and she loved him. 'That should get me through the evening,' she said.

'Who is he?'

'I don't know really. Something to do with business, only my father isn't here and I'm stuck with him on my own for now.'

'Old chap?'

'Thirties.'

'I think I'll ring you later,' said Jeremy. 'Just to make sure the fangs haven't developed, because from what I remember of the films Dracula gets the girls.'

'Not this girl,' she gurgled. 'I can promise you that. I'm not to his taste.'

'I'll still ring.'

That might not be a good idea tonight, not after this morning, not until she had talked to her father. But by the end of dinner she could need another little chat with Jeremy, so she said, 'Better if I ring you. What are you doing after the show?'

'Going back to the flat.'

She heard her father's car and said quickly, 'My father's home. I will ring you.'

'See you do. I don't like the sound of Dracula.'

'You think I do?' She was still smiling when she hurried outside. Her father didn't see her right away. The two retrievers had dashed out to welcome him, and although he stopped to pat them, there was no exuberance in his movements. He was an athletic man. He played golf, tennis, an occasional game of squash, but tonight he seemed to Charlotte to be moving slowly as he came across the courtyard from the garages.

She went to meet him feeling guilty. He was tired. He had had a long day. Charlotte said, 'Hello, love,' and slipped her hand through his arm. 'Am I glad to see you!

Aunt Lucy will be too, you know how she is about meals getting spoiled.'

'I'm not that late, surely.'

'You've just made it.'

'You've met Saul?'

'Er—yes.' She would have liked to get a few more details about the man, but her father was hurrying now, telling her, 'I'll be with you in five minutes. You just keep him entertained.'

Bring on the dancing girls, she thought. She said, 'He isn't easy company.'

At the bottom of the stairs her father said, 'Just talk to him, there's a good girl,' and rebellion stirred in her.

'I don't think he wants to talk to me. He thinks I'm rather stupid.'

'Only in some matters,' said her father, and smiled, patting her cheek, and she thought, I'm forgiven for this morning, but he meant it. Not just about not helping the theatre but about Jeremy.

'About this morning——' she began.

'Sorry,' he said. 'The answer's the same.' He didn't give her time to explain that she had wanted to apologise. She had hardly expected him to change his mind, just like that, but she would have to prove him wrong.

Her heart told her that Jeremy was the man for her, just as surely as her nerves jangled when she was near Saul Laurenson. As soon as she opened the drawing room door, and saw him sitting where she'd left him, she felt that tightening in her throat.

'You've had your word with Lucy?' His voice was pleasant enough, deep and crisp; and what with the phone call and talking to her father she had been away quite a time. She would have smiled at almost any other man and asked, 'Did you miss me?' She said to Saul, 'My

father's here.' Then she sat down and waited to see if he
would say anything.

At this time of evening there was hardly any sound. It
was too early for the night creatures and the day birds
had stopped twittering. Very little traffic came down this
road, but Charlotte heard the grandfather clock strike in
the hall, and a door shut somewhere.

It seemed hours, sitting there, although it was in fact
rather less than two minutes, before her nerve cracked and
she jumped up and asked, 'Would you mind if I turned
on the television? It's one of my favourite programmes.'

'Not at all.'

It would give her something to listen to, and something
else to look at, because it was hard to sit alone in your
own drawing room with a strange man without looking at
him. He was tall and lean, dark crescent-shaped eyebrows,
aquiline nose, slightly sunken cheeks. If he had been
wearing a black cloak, scarlet-lined, over that dark suit,
he would have made a chillingly saturnine Dracula. He
had the mouth for it too, strong and sensual, and that was
when she switched on the TV.

She found herself with a choice between football, a
heavily slanted political programme, and an old Western,
and stayed with the movie. Guns were blazing away when
her father came into the room and asked, 'Is anybody
watching this?'

'I'm a Clint Eastwood fan,' said Charlotte.

'I didn't know that,' said her father. He turned off the
television, apologising for delaying dinner, and hoped that
Charlotte had been entertaining the guest.

'Yes indeed,' said Saul Laurenson, and she thought, A
circus act and a strip-tease, what more could you ask?
This was part of her duties, providing the womanly touch
in her father's home, and usually she enjoyed it. But Saul
Laurenson made her feel clumsy and stupid, so that she

could hardly dish up without clattering spoons and she only just avoided spilling her wine, fingering the stem of her glass.

Aunt Lucy ate with them in the evenings if it was only Charlotte and her father, or if the guests were old friends. But tonight she came in and left the food, and Georgy edged in with her, realised the stranger was still here, yelped and shot off; and for the first time Charlotte felt a real affinity with him. That was what she would have liked to do—yelp and run.

It was a sultry evening. It would have been nice if they could have opened the windows wide, but that would have brought the moths fluttering in, and Saul Laurenson certainly seemed cool enough. Charlotte had to admit that he was a striking man, but just looking at him made her feel uncomfortable.

She found it almost impossible to join in the conversation. He and her father seemed to know each other well, although she had never heard of him before. It wasn't 'shop' talk, it was mostly about local properties that were for sale. It seemed that Laurenson was considering buying a house round here.

Her father tried to draw her into the talk. 'You know the black-and-white house down by the river in Tiddington,' he'd say. 'That's coming on the market.' But apart from saying,

'I think I know the one you mean. It seems very attractive,' she was struck dumb, and she knew it was because she was scared of making a fool of herself again if she opened her mouth.

He was so maddeningly superior. Oh, he sounded amusing and charming, there was nothing patronising about his manner, but she would have staked her life that he was expecting her to behave like an idiot. He waited for her to speak, when her father addressed her, and the words died on her lips. All through the meal she offered no more than a murmur or a brief sentence. She never said anything informative or funny or even half-way bright.

And she knew that her father was disappointed in her. He thought she was sulking. She never had sulked, but nothing had ever been denied her before, and she had a headache building up. That was another rare occurrence for her. It must be something to do with the thunder in the air, but the back of her neck was stiff and tender and sharp little darts were stabbing her eyes. So that from time to time she looked away from the table, and the two men seated there, trying to still the mounting tempo of pain.

It didn't help much and, as Lucy brought in the dessert, Charlotte said, 'Would it be terribly rude if I said good-night to you both, but I do have this splitting headache?' Her father looked surprised, he probably didn't believe her, and she muttered apologetically, 'It's true—I do. I think there's going to be a storm.'

Outside the dining room Aunt Lucy said, 'You do look a bit washed out,' and Charlotte fanned herself with her hand.

'That was one of the worst meals I have ever sat through. Oh, not your cooking, love, the food was delicious, but Mr Saul Laurenson gives me acute indigestion!'

'That's a pity,' said Aunt Lucy. 'Because he'll be spoiling your breakfast as well. He's staying the night.'

'Nobody told me.' But her father had told Aunt Lucy and there was always a guest room ready, and although the Blue Boar was only five miles away it was never wise to drive and drink. But Charlotte wanted him out of the house. She said, 'Well, I'll have my breakfast in the kitchen. Have you got any aspirins?'

The aspirins stopped it getting worse. She lay on her

bed, fully dressed with her eyes closed, trying to relax for a while. She imagined herself at the theatre, watching Jeremy. She had seen several rehearsals and she had a good memory, she could remember most of the script, so she went over Jeremy's speeches in her head, and then she daydreamed herself going back to his flat with him, walking hand in hand through the warm dark night.

The flat was nothing special. It was over a fish and chip shop and he shared it with another actor, and once he had said, 'Wouldn't it be fantastic if I could be coming home to you at nights? If we had a little place, the two of us.'

They had only been talking nonsense, but sometimes since then Charlotte had seen apartments or small houses advertised, or passed For Sale notices, and thought, I wish I was the kind of girl who could just move in like that and set up home with a man. Some day she might, but right now it was all dreaming.

She gave Jeremy time to get back to the flat, then she rang him and he answered at once. 'Any sign of the fangs?' he asked.

'I'm thinking of going in for a blood count in the morning. He drains me.'

'You know, I find that hard to believe.'

Charlotte was a vivid personality, an extrovert. Saul Laurenson was the first man she had met who had given her an inferiority complex, but now she said wistfully, 'I wish you could get over here for an hour or two. Believe it or not, I'm in urgent need of support.'

If she drove away someone in the house would probably hear her car, or she would have gone before now. 'I'm on my way,' said Jeremy, 'but how's your old man going to receive me?'

'Don't come to the house. Drive down the track and park on the verge and walk over to the patio. I'll be waiting for you.'

'On my way,' he said again.

Charlotte left Georgy in her bedroom, where he slept on the rug beside her bed. She could do without him panicking at shadows in the garden, and she crept down the back stairs and out of the house. The other dogs were in the kitchen. So, probably, was Aunt Lucy. The men were most likely in the drawing room where her father would be puffing away on a cigar, although his old friend and doctor had warned him to cut down his smoking. 'If it's reached the stage where a man can't enjoy a quiet cigar,' her father would say, 'we've reached a pretty pass,' and Dr Buckston would sigh and shake his head as her father cut the end off another Havana.

Charlotte wondered what they were talking about and hurried until the trees shielded her from the drawing room windows, because she was suddenly scared that Saul Laurenson might be standing where he could see the lawns, and pick out her white dress in the moonlight. She didn't feel safe until she was well into the trees.

Then she sat in the little summerhouse, waiting for Jeremy, and it was all very romantic. This had probably happened to other girls in her family, and to girls who had worked in the house in the old days. Sometimes the moon made everything bright as day, including the marble hound-dog and the lumpy little concrete peke. At other time when clouds hid the moon the night was shadowed and mysterious.

She heard the sound of the car engine and went to meet Jeremy across the field, running because she really did need his reassurance. The force of her greeting flattered and surprised him. He wrapped his arms around her, and asked, 'Hey, what is all this? You're really shaken, aren't you?'

He looked very like the hero of a romance, tall, and

handsome, and she said, 'I'm just so glad to see you. I'm not shaken, I just had to get away.'

They walked back to the little summerhouse, arms around each other's waists, and Jeremy told her how the performance had gone tonight. The girl playing Phoebe had fluffed her lines again, but he had carried on, getting round the impasse, and Charlotte said, 'Oh, you're so clever, you're far and away the best they've got.'

He agreed with her. 'Bless you,' he said. 'But what about this man, what's he been doing to my girl?'

'Nothing at all, but when he looks at me I want to do a Georgy and run.'

Jeremy cupped her face with his hands, looking down at her. 'You're not usually so impressionable. You don't fancy him, do you?'

She gave a muted shriek. 'Never in a million years!'

'That's all right, then. Oh God, you're so beautiful.' His voice throbbed, just like it did on the stage, and he started kissing her. As his lips feathered across her cheek-bones, and she felt herself melting deliciously, she suddenly wondered how Saul Laurenson would make love.

She had no idea where that thought came from, but it acted like cold water on her emotional responses, so that she kissed Jeremy back pretty briskly and then said, 'I was thinking it might not be a bad idea if you came along for a meal. On Sunday perhaps, if you've nothing else on. I know my father's going to like you once he gets to know you and over Aunt Lucy's cooking he's usually in a mellow mood.'

'Well, I'm prepared to put myself out.' Jeremy grinned, in disarmingly boyish fashion. 'It matters to you, doesn't it?'

'Him liking you? Of course it does, I'd hate to hurt him.'

'Look, sweetheart,' he stroked the tumbling waves of her hair, 'suppose we don't win him round—rich men with gorgeous daughters can be very pigheaded—and suppose we did decide to give marriage a try, how do you think he'd react in the long run?'

This was the first time they had spoken of marriage. It thrilled her, hearing Jeremy say the word, but at the same time she didn't take the blatant hint because this was all supposing. And they would win her father round, so there was no need to rush into anything. She said, 'Come to lunch on Sunday and let's start from there.'

'It's a date.' He drew her close and kissed her again, and she kissed him too and thought how much she loved him and how beautiful it was out here. Then she heard Tria barking and coming closer and stiffened in Jeremy's embrace.

'The dogs are out.'

'So?' he said. 'You do mean your household pets, don't you?'

'Tria and Wilbur. But my father's probably strolling around with them—he often does. I don't want him finding you here. I said I had a headache and I was going to bed.'

'Heck, no,' Jeremy agreed, and looked around for some concealment. The obvious thing to do was to hide between the trees, but Charlotte added,

'I'd better walk back to the house with him. The dogs are going to make for me, they'll find me, and I can always say I came out for a breath of air, but he isn't going to leave me here without getting suspicious.'

'What if the dogs make for me?'

The barking was getting nearer all the time. She said, 'You'd better go, I'll see you lunchtime tomorrow. They wouldn't hurt you, they're two old softies, but it might be awkward.'

'It would.' Jeremy went without kissing her goodbye, although he did whisper, 'I love you,' as he hurried off. That was the sensible thing to do, it was what she had suggested herself, so it was unreasonable of her to feel that he could hardly have moved faster if Tria and Wilbur had been a couple of bloodhounds.

She stayed where she was until the two retrievers came with swishing tails into the clearing of the patio, then she walked out of the summerhouse towards them as they bounded up. 'Hello, you two,' she said.

Clouds were partly obscuring the moon, but her father was with the dogs. She couldn't hear him, but she could see the shape of a man through the trees, and suddenly it went darker still and a little cold breeze touched her, and she called, 'Father?'

It had been lovely down here, as safe as the house, and Tria and Wilbur were snuffling carefree, but as Saul Laurenson stepped out Charlotte's heart missed a couple of beats. He seemed to be part of the darkness, and he moved like a panther. He was alone, her father wasn't behind him, and her heart was making up for lost beats and going so fast and hard that she could feel it thumping inside her. She thought, I shall choke. She thought, If he touches me I shall run screaming all the way back to the house.

'Headache better?' he enquired.

'What?' She had been in two minds whether to dodge past him and make a break for it without saying a word. That was how he panicked her, and what a fool she would have been if she had. 'Much better, thank you,' she said, her voice clipped but controlled.

The cloud floated clear and moonlight streamed down, and she was conscious of her own dishevelment. Her hair was falling all over the place, for one thing, and one of her shoulder straps had slipped and she was breathing fast. The sound of a car engine starting up was loud in the silence, and Saul Laurenson said gravely, 'Surprising what the night air can do.'

He knew she hadn't been out here alone. He thought that headache had been an excuse, which it had, although it had been real enough and if she didn't get away from him it would be back in full force. She said, 'Isn't it?' and called to the dogs and almost ran back to the house.

Where *was* her father? Not only did Saul Laurenson have the run of the house, he had the run of the gardens too, it seemed, and he had chosen just that moment to stroll in the direction of the patio and make her look a fool for the third time. He certainly had a talent for being where she didn't want him to be, and as soon as she woke next morning she thought, Today I'm keeping out of his way.

He had stayed the night, but of course he would be leaving after breakfast, and when she got her father alone she would explain. It had never happened before, she always got on well with people, so she could surely say, 'Just this once, just this man—I don't want to be around if he's coming here again.'

She was usually downstairs not much after Aunt Lucy. Aunt Lucy was a naturally early riser, who couldn't be persuaded to lie in. 'Best time of the day,' she'd say, bustling around at seven o'clock; which indeed it probably is in the summer, but even on dark winter mornings she was up and about. To make up for this she tended to nod in front of the TV after ten o'clock at night, but until the ten o'clock news she was indefatigable.

This morning Charlotte waited until she heard a car leave, before she came down the back stairs into the kitchen and asked, 'Is the coast clear?'

'If you mean Mr Laurenson,' said Aunt Lucy, 'that was him just now. Your father hasn't gone yet, though. I think he's waiting for you. He's sitting a long time over his breakfast, but he isn't eating much.'

Her father was still at the table, with a newspaper open, and half a cup of coffee at his elbow. The toast rack seemed untouched and he didn't usually linger over breakfast, so Charlotte said, 'Sorry I'm late.'

'You missed our guest,' said her father reproachfully.

'I know.' She poured herself coffee and wrinkled her nose and tried to make him smile. 'But after dinner I didn't much fancy having breakfast with him.'

'Whatever got into you last night?' Her father wasn't smiling, and she sat on the table's edge and took a gulp of coffee before she tried to explain.

'I don't like him. He bothers me. I seem to behave like an idiot when he's around. Did he tell you I jumped the hedge when he was driving up the track and nearly landed on his car?'

'No, he didn't tell me.' She could have made a funny story of that, and a funnier one about coming in from sunbathing and losing her bra, and usually it took hardly anything to make her father chuckle. But this morning his face was set in heavy lines, so that she instinctively went to smooth the frown from his forehead.

'I don't have to be friends with him, do I?' she wheedled, stroking his brow. 'I don't have to see him. Surely there's no reason I should be around if he comes here again.'

'Sit down,' said her father. He gestured at a chair, and Charlotte sat down abruptly because her knees started to give when he went on, 'And I'll tell you a very good reason why you and I will be seeing a very great deal of Saul Laurenson in the future.'

CHAPTER THREE

WHEN her father said, 'Money,' Charlotte wasn't surprised. She had known that Saul Laurenson's presence here had something to do with the business, but when her father went on, 'The Little Theatre isn't the only place feeling the pinch these days,' she exclaimed incredulously, 'Not us?'

'Why not us? We're in a luxury trade and luxuries are getting hit.' Colin Dunscombe's voice was heavily ironic. 'There's no divine intervention for jewellers.'

Charlotte knew nothing about the financial side of Dunscombes, but she took prosperity for granted. Their life-style had always been luxurious and there had been no sign that it was about to change. But she knew in her bones that Saul Laurenson was no ordinary man, no ordinary visitor. When he was near she felt threatened. She asked now, 'How does he come into it?'

'He's a rich man,' said her father. 'And a very astute one. We need his backing, my love, I don't want you antagonising him.'

She hadn't been the antagoniser. She was the one who had to get out of the room because he was giving her a headache. She asked, 'How long have you known him?'

'Some time.'

'But not as a personal friend. Not close. He's never been here.'

'No, but now he's interested in the business and he's considering buying a house in the Cotswolds.'

The Cotswolds covered a wide area. He might live miles away, their paths might never cross. But if he became involved in Dunscombes it could be a different matter; and if he was house-hunting here it looked as though he intended keeping an eye on any investment.

'Is he married?' She hadn't asked before, although it was a question that usually came up soon after meeting anyone, whether you were interested in the reply or not.

She could imagine him with a high fashion wife, somebody very elegant. No, she thought at once, I can't. With girl-friends, but not a wife. I don't believe he's a man who would commit himself to one woman.

'He isn't married,' said her father.

'I don't know why I asked you that. I really don't want to know anything about him.' She jumped from her perch on the table's edge and began to pace around the room, nervous as a cat in strange surroundings. 'I never met anybody before that I disliked so much, and now you tell me I've got to make up to him. You know, I don't think I can do that. I feel so edgy when I'm near him that I know if I open my mouth I shall say something idiotic.

'If you want him to invest in the business and he wants to that's splendid, I suppose, but I don't really want to see him again. I don't suppose I made much of an impression on him last night, but he made a big impression on me. Just sitting at the same table with him gave me a headache—like thunder in the air, you know, before a storm.'

'Don't over-dramatise.' Her father sounded weary and she was piling on the agony. 'You're getting bad habits from your theatrical friends. All I'm asking you to do is behave in a civilised fashion. You were sulking like a child last night. I've never known you to carry on like that before.'

He was shocked and disappointed in her, and she had been childish. She asked, in a rush of contrition, 'What do you want me to do?'

'There are several properties Saul's looking over today, I said you'd go with him.'

'Me?' she squeaked. 'Why me?'

'Because you've lived in the Cotswolds all your life.' He gave a small wry smile. 'Because I thought you'd enjoy it.'

Charlotte did enjoy looking round houses. She had helped several of her friends when they were house-hunting, and she would have been delighted to go along with anyone else. But the thought of spending most of the day with Saul Laurenson was a daunting one.

'I don't——' she began to protest, then her conscience took over. It was no big thing. If the recession was beginning to bite she must help in every way she could. She said, 'All right, if I go along what do you want me to do?'

'Give your opinion if you're asked for it.' He drained the coffee in his cup, although it looked cold, got up and said, 'I'll see you later. He's at the Blue Boar in Chipping Queanton, he's expecting you about half past nine.'

Charlotte couldn't see Saul Laurenson asking for her opinion. Her father must have volunteered her company, because she was sure it wasn't Laurenson's idea, and although she still had three-quarters of an hour to kill she had no appetite for breakfast.

She walked Georgy round the garden, then left him in the care of Aunt Lucy. 'I'm going house-hunting,' she explained, 'with Mr Laurenson, who's decided he'd like to live around here, and he scares me, so he'd probably give Georgy convulsions before we were through.'

'Scares you?' Aunt Lucy was in the drawing room, dusting a plump white porcelain Cupid. 'Why should he scare you?'

'I don't know,' Charlotte admitted as Aunt Lucy replaced the Cupid on the shelf of a corner cupboard. 'Except that my father says we could use his backing in the business, and that scares me because I think he might take over.'

'Your father knows what he's doing,' said Aunt Lucy. 'Don't you fret.' She went on with her dusting and Charlotte said, 'Of course he does.' But she was convinced that Saul Laurenson was a ruthless man, and the prospect of getting into his debt scared her sick . . .

The Blue Boar Hotel, which had once been a small manor house, was on the outskirts of town. The coat of arms of the defunct family, painted in bold bright colours above the great stone fireplace in the main hall, sported a blue boar. Charlotte gave her name and Saul Laurenson's to the clerk at the reception desk and got an admiring smile in return.

Some men had all the luck, the clerk decided. Not only was Mr Laurenson obviously rolling in money—he'd booked into the best suite in the hotel—but he had this fantastic bird after him. Class she was too, anyone could see that.

'Ask her to come up,' said Saul Laurenson when he was informed that Miss Dunscombe had arrived, and the clerk passed on the message with instructions how to reach the master-suite.

Charlotte would have loved to say, 'Tell him to come down,' and seat herself in one of the leather armchairs and let Saul Laurenson do the running. But she wasn't to antagonise him, so she smiled and said, 'Thank you,' and took the stairs rather than the little gilt birdcage of a lift. With her luck, when he was around, the lift would probably have stuck between floors, and he would have watched her being hauled out like a sack of potatoes.

He answered the door when she tapped on it. Today he wore an open-necked beige shirt and a beige jacket of thin supple chamois. Casual dress, with dark brown slacks, but he looked no more approachable than he had in last night's formal suit. His smile was nothing like the clerk's bright-eyed admiring grin, although after he had said, 'Good morning,' he did add, 'This is very civil of you.'

Charlotte shrugged, 'Looking at houses is no trouble,' as she stepped into a sitting room, attractively furnished, period pieces combined with comfortable chairs and a TV set concealed in a corner cupboard. Some papers on a round inlaid table looked like estate agents' circulars.

'Perhaps you'd like to glance at those,' he suggested as he went through another door, leaving it open.

She raised her voice to ask, 'What do you want me to tell you? If they're in residential areas or if a river's likely to rise? I mean, you can see those kind of things for yourself, can't you?'

'Maybe, but local knowledge can be very useful in property buying.'

When she didn't see him she found it easier to talk to him. 'Why do you want to live round here?' she asked.

'Beautiful countryside, don't you agree?'

Of course she agreed, but her father thought that the business and the decision to buy a house went together, and she picked up the top sheet of paper and whistled at the price and said, 'It's a lot to be spending to put a roof over your head.' He'd get super luxury for this kind of money, and she thought of Jeremy's little flat, half a flat as he was sharing, and it didn't seem fair.

'Is that how you would describe a home? Your own, for instance?' Saul Laurenson was back in the room, a brief-case under his arm. Charlotte didn't look at him again after a first quick glance, but he went on looking at her and her small Georgian home was in the upper income bracket and she had no call to be snide about what he was prepared to pay.

'Talking of money,' he said, 'I presume your father's mentioned our business discussions?'

She nodded, although all she knew was that Saul Laurenson was rich and astute and Dunscombes had need of him. She said slowly, 'We've always been a family business. I should hate to see an outsider join us.'

'Today's economic climate makes strange bedfellows.' Before she could stop herself she had spat out,

'I hope you don't imagine you're speaking literally,' and could have bitten her tongue, because of course he laughed and said, 'Nothing was further from my mind. Shall we go?'

His car was drawn up in front of the hotel, hers was in the parking area behind, and as they walked through the main entrance she asked, 'Whose car are we taking? I know all the short cuts. Shall I drive?'

He declined promptly, 'No, thank you, you might drive like you ride.' He opened the passenger door for her and she muttered,

'I'm as good a rider as you're likely to come across, matey.' She hadn't expected him to hear, he was walking around to get into the driving seat, but as he settled himself in he said,

'I'm sure you are, but you do have this little habit of not looking where you're going. Fasten your seat-belt.'

She had been about to do just that, but her fingers stiffened and she sat back, announcing, 'I prefer to feel free.' No way would she do what he told her. He didn't argue. She didn't think he did much arguing. She could imagine him giving orders in crisp incisive tones: Do this. Do that. This is how the situation will be handled. And she remembered him sitting at her father's desk in her father's study, and she visualised him in her father's office at Dunscombe's, and thought, oh lord, I hope I'm not psychic. I hope it could never come true.

She said suddenly, 'I don't have anything to do with the financial side of the business. I'm a designer.'

'Of course you are,' he said. He didn't believe she worked, but she *did* have talent even if he reckoned she was of no value to the firm. Oh, she *wished* they didn't need him, and tonight she must ask her father exactly what the position was and how Saul Laurenson was likely to feature in her future.

The car was coming to the traffic lights and the theatre. She had told Jeremy she would see him today, he would be expecting her around lunchtime. Now she might not make it, and she sighed, taking advantage of the red signal to look up and down the pavement, checking passers-by. This was where he worked, he might be coming or going.

But he wasn't, and Saul Laurenson was watching her, so she said, 'It's a theatre,' which was obvious.

'So I see,' he said, and as the lights changed and the car moved, 'Do you act?'

'It isn't an amateur theatre, it's a very good professional one. They put on some marvellous shows. While you're here you should go and see one of them.'

Then she spotted Jeremy's flatmate coming out of the small supermarket, with both arms around a loaded carrier bag, and began to wind down the window. 'Can't you stop?' she asked, and yelled, 'Peter!'

'Not here I can't.' There wasn't an inch of parking space and the traffic was moving in a steady stream.

'Peter!' she bellowed, getting her head through the window and attracting the attention of the crowds but not of the portly bearded actor ambling along with his groceries.

'A pity you're not on the stage,' remarked Saul Laurenson, 'you'd have no trouble making them hear up in the gallery. Is your friend deaf?'

'Seems like it. *Damn!*' She could have given Peter a message and Jeremy wouldn't have hung around waiting for her to turn up. She flopped back in her seat with an exasperated grunt, and Saul Laurenson turned left down a side street, drew up and said,

'If you don't mind running after him now's your chance.'

'Thanks.' She was out of the car, dodging pedestrians, haring down the main road until she could reach out and grab Peter's arm. 'Peter, hi! Give Jeremy a message for me, will you?' She gasped for a few seconds, getting her breath. 'Tell him I can't make lunch but I'll ring him this evening, would you do that?'

'For you, my beauty, anything.' Peter Stubbs leered at her and she said,

'You are nice. I've got to fly. I just hopped out of a car round the corner.'

Saul, double-parked, was talking to a policeman, and Charlotte thought, That's done it, I've got him booked! Then she realised from the policeman's gestures that Saul was being given directions, and as she walked up Saul said, 'Let me see if I've got it. First left, second right, straight on till I come to the Public Library and then . . .'

Charlotte went on walking. The car passed her before the first turning and she hurried after it. He was waiting outside the Library, and as she ran up he opened the door and she got in gasping, 'I thought he was booking you.'

'It was a near thing. Did you catch up with Peter?'

'Yes, thank you.'

'All satisfactory now?'

'Thank you, yes.'

'It didn't take long.'

'Just as well,' she said. If he had to drive off and leave her she wouldn't have minded, and she was sure he wouldn't. She didn't like his grin and she said tartly, 'He didn't hear me call after him, you know. He wasn't avoiding me.'

'What man would?' he murmured, and she knew he was sending her up and she didn't appreciate his sense of humour.

'Anyway,' she muttered, 'I only wanted him to give somebody a message. I had a date for lunch that I can't keep now I don't have a car, and I probably won't be able to get a taxi, and I can't be sure of getting back here by one o'clock.'

'I apologise,' he said gravely. 'You should have explained that this was interfering with your plans.'

'It doesn't matter.' She was here and she had to be civil. 'Well,' she went on, 'it's a nice day for house-hunting.' That was pretty trite, but he agreed, 'It's a nice day for almost anything,' and Charlotte thought, so who cares if he thinks I'm dumb? It was better than being tonguetied like last night. She asked, 'Where are we going first?'

The address was about five miles away. Two houses were being built in what had been a meadow. Behind them rose green dappled hills where sheep grazed, and it was altogether a pleasant pastoral setting.

One house was almost completed, the other was in an earlier stage of construction with builders still at work. As their car drew up a man came to meet them, beaming from ear to ear. 'Mr Laurenson? *Good* morning.' He gave Charlotte the look she expected, tribute to her beauty, but respectful because she was with the man who had come to inspect this very pricey property.

The estate agent began his spiel at once, pointing out the open views, the weathered tiles and bricks, the genuine old oak door. It was a new house fashioned from materials cannibalised from demolitions. When the churned-up rock-hard earth around had been cultivated into a garden these houses were going to look as though they had been here for anything up to a hundred years.

Inside the staircase was of fumed oak and the hall was

flagstoned. 'Perhaps the lady would like to see the kitchens,' the estate agent suggested. 'Apart from the overhead beams they are, of course, completely modern.'

Charlotte didn't want to be taken into what might become Saul Laurenson's kitchen by a man who thought she might be doing the cooking there. 'The lady,' she said, 'would like to wander around if she may.' Alone, she would enjoy this. It was a charming house, a bit of a cheat, but what did that matter when the old materials were so beautiful? These doors and staircase could have ended up on a demolition bonfire. A little while ago they would have done, but now nostalgia was coming into its own and most of the people she knew would be happy living here.

Saul went off with the estate agent and she wandered into another room, playing her game of pretending that she was shopping for a home for herself and Jeremy. This would be wonderful, near enough to the theatre and Dunscombes, not too far from her father. If only a couple of noughts were knocked off the price this would be perfect.

She went poking around in cupboards, passing the men from time to time but doing her best to dodge them, ending in a bedroom at the back that would look over the garden and the hills. Roses would grow well, foxgloves, poppies, wild flowers. She would like to make a garden from the bare earth. She would like to make a home.

A walnut tree grew at the far limits of the 'garden' and she would put a bench under that where they could sit on warm evenings, like tonight would be, and she could listen to Jeremy learning his lines, read out other parts and help him. Then they would come up here together. She closed her eyes, hands clasped together, and thought, I love you, my love; I wish you were with me now.

She was so deep in her dreaming that she didn't hear

the footsteps, but she felt the touch on her shoulder and her heart leapt into her mouth. For a wild moment she half expected to see Jeremy, but it was Saul, of course, and shock jerked her against him, colour draining from her face as she gasped, 'Oh, lordy, you frightened me! I didn't hear you coming, I was miles away.'

She wished she was, instead of being held between his steadying hands. Finding herself so close to him, with his hands on her, was like being torn out of Jeremy's arms, all her senses ran amok. She didn't know how she was feeling or what she was saying. She leaned back against the window frame and began to babble, 'I didn't hear you, I was planning a garden out there and I got a bit involved. My head's swimming.'

'Do you get many headaches?'

'It isn't aching, it's swimming—I never get headaches.' Except last night. 'Except last night,' she corrected herself. 'And it's hot in here and I came out without breakfast.'

She was getting herself together fairly fast now that he had stopped holding her. He had strange eyes, dark enough for Dracula. It was all of a piece, his face. Some men had thick fierce eyebrows and weak mouths, or lovely mouths and shifty eyes. But there wasn't a weak feature in Saul Laurenson's face. The lines, of laughter and thought, were deep, and the mouth was hard. But it wasn't a thin-lipped mouth, she had noticed that before.

They were alone, she noticed that now, and asked, 'Where's the man who's doing the selling?'

'Gone back to his office.'

'What——' She had to stop to moisten her dry lips. 'What do you think of it?'

'I'd like to see others,' he said, and she went on chattering, 'New houses feel empty, don't they?' Of course they did when they were empty. 'Strange,' she added. 'Echoing. You have to put your own imprint on them.'

She had imagined herself down there in the garden, and in this room, with Jeremy, but now she couldn't see Jeremy for Saul. For a disloyal moment she felt that he might dominate Jeremy, even if Jeremy was an actor, trained for and loving the spotlight.

'Where now?' she asked.

'There's a flat in Stratford.' Six miles away. 'And then we'll look around for lunch. If you skipped breakfast, and I've ruined your date, the least I can do is feed you.'

Charlotte started to say, 'Well, thanks, but I'm not really hungry,' when her tummy gave a hollow rumble and she grinned instead and said, 'I think I'm getting a message.'

The men on the scaffolding next door got a better look at her this time, and set up a chorus of wolf whistles. She laughed and as she climbed into the car called across, 'I think you're building two super houses.'

'You're a pretty super build yourself!' one shouted back, and Saul closed her door and got into the driving seat and she wondered if his silence meant disapproval or simply lack of interest.

The flat was a penthouse overlooking the river, very luxurious in every way, furnished by the present occupants, who were abroad so that again they were conducted around by an estate agent, and again Charlotte removed herself from the men and did her own rambling and dreaming. She could imagine Jeremy here all right, but the trouble was that Saul *was* here. His voice seemed to carry, no matter how hard she tried not to listen, and when she couldn't see him she could feel him like vibrations in the air. He was too powerful a personality by half.

She came downstairs and stood by the car and watched the river until he joined her. 'Getting bored?' he asked.

'No, it's a highly desirable residence. I'd like it. I'd

like the last one too.'

'You planning on leaving home?'

She said, 'No, but nothing stays the same for ever.'
Nothing stayed the same from day to day. The day before
yesterday she had been happy and secure, then came the
row with her father and she had learned that the business
was in trouble and Saul Laurenson had cast his shadow
over her life. She added with fervour, 'More's the pity.'

'Changes can be for the better.'

'Promises, promises,' she said flippantly and gaily, and
he sat back in the driving seat, and looked at her with
eyes as black as pitch, and said softly, 'But I'm not prom-
ising you anything,' and a cold shiver ran down her spine
and she thought, It's true all right, I am scared of him . . .

They went into a hotel, ordered food, ate. The dining
room was full and Charlotte chattered animatedly, trying
to entertain. She felt she was cutting no ice with Saul, but
then she didn't like him either, so it evened out, and her
reflection in a mirror on the wall showed her a radiantly
pretty girl, and she drank two glasses of sparkling wine
and took comfort in the fact that there was only one more
house to see. Then she could go home and phone Jeremy.

'I have to make a phone call,' said Saul, checking his
watch. 'Will you excuse me?'

Indefinitely, Charlotte thought, don't you hurry back
for me. 'Of course,' she said, and watched him go through
the door and ate a little more of her rum baba, then
decided this would be an opportune time to slip to the
loo. The toilets were just beyond the phones. Saul had his
back to her, they were the semi-open booths, and she
could hear what he was saying.

He was telling someone about the properties they had
viewed this morning, and having passed him and rounded
the corner she couldn't resist lingering. He might mention
Dunscombes, and she was dying to know what was going

on there, so she stood as near as she could remaining hidden, straining to hear, hoping that nobody would come along and catch her eavesdropping.

He said a few more words about the penthouse flat, about the lease, then he laughed. 'Oh, she's beautiful all right,' he said, 'and dumb as they come. She must have an I.Q. in single figures,' and she choked.

He was talking about *her*. Somebody was laughing with him, without a doubt, and she nearly marched right back and stopped them laughing. She did take a step before she checked herself. She shouldn't have heard that, Saul had named no names, what could she *say*? He might go on laughing, he might think this was hilarious.

She dived into the Ladies' and glared at her reflection which had turned very white. Dumb as they come ... I.Q. in single figures ... I could murder him, she thought, who the hell is he telling that to? She was shaking with rage so that a woman, emerging from the loo, enquired anxiously if she was all right.

'Yes, thank you,' Charlotte managed to croak.

'It's the heat,' said the woman. 'I can't stand it myself. Why don't you sit down?'

Charlotte sat down. What cheek, she kept thinking, what *flaming* cheek! Who does he think he is, Mastermind? 'Would you like an aspirin?' the woman offered, digging into her handbag and coming up with a strip of tablets. She tore off a couple and Charlotte thanked her, although it wasn't aspirins she needed. Now she could have used a cyanide pill, she could have dropped that in Saul Laurenson's coffee.

She took a long deep breath to stop the shaking, and came out of the Ladies' still glittering with fury. She'd show him! What was his I.Q., she'd like to know?

He was no longer at the phone but back at the table, and she took her place opposite and smiled at him with tight lips. Right, she thought, let's have some intelligent conversation; and she launched into a dissertation on party politics. It wasn't one of her favourite subjects, but local problems and local politics always got an airing in the local papers, and she had a retentive memory.

Saul listened, asking the occasional question that she either answered or skirted, and then she went on to national and international news, quoting shamelessly from articles she had read, looking and sounding earnest and erudite.

She gave quite a performance, until a sip of the sparkling rosé wine went down the wrong way and started her choking. When she had finished spluttering she looked across at Saul, through streaming eyes, and he was grinning.

'It doesn't take much to amuse you, does it?' she snapped.

'Sorry,' his lips were still twitching, 'but I'll upgrade you into two figures, possibly even three.'

'What?'

'Your I.Q.'

She nearly choked again. Instead she gulped and glared, 'You knew I heard that!' He must have seen her pass and guessed she would stop just round the corner and eavesdrop. He had been leading her on.

'Haven't you heard that listeners never hear any good of themselves?' he said, eyes glinting with amusement, and Charlotte would have loved to empty the dregs of the wine bottle over his head.

'Don't put me down, damn you!' she gritted, clenching her hands on the table so that her knuckles shone, and he shook a reprovingly head,

'Temper, temper.' It was a long time since her temper had flared like this and she unclenched her fingers and tried to smile. She managed a half-hearted grin, 'At any rate, you said I was beautiful.'

'Very beautiful. You must get told that often.'

'Sometimes.' It would have been hypocrisy to pretend she wasn't used to flattery, but Saul Laurenson was no more moved by her face than by the aquamarine ring on her finger. They were both beautiful, but not rare enough in his world to impress him. She said, 'I'm not so dumb, you know.'

'I never thought you were.'

The admission made her smile naturally. 'All right,' she said, 'I shouldn't have hung around listening. I don't make a habit of eavesdropping, I promise you, but I am curious to hear just what you're planning for the family firm.'

'Ask your father.'

'Oh, I will,' she said, 'I will.' She might have tried to get a little information from Saul—although she was pretty sure he considered the subject closed—but just then she heard her name called.

Jo-Ann Marley had known Charlotte ever since they were children. She had blonde bubble curls, a very pretty face and a hungry eye for the men. It was Charlotte's escort, rather than Charlotte herself, who brought Jo-Ann over. She was lunching with a couple of aunts, and bored with them, when she spotted Charlotte, and then Saul. 'Back in a minute,' she told the aunts. 'Charlotte!' she called, and her brilliant smile started with Charlotte but quickly switched to Saul, although she was speaking to Charlotte.

'Hello, stranger,' she gurgled. 'Ages since I've seen you.'

Not really, thought Charlotte. Not more than a few weeks. She said, 'Hello, this is Saul Laurenson; Saul, Jo-Ann Marley.'

'We went to school together,' Jo-Ann gurgled.

'Charlotte was the clever one. She still is, isn't she? I'm stuck with two old aunts and here she is with yet another feller. By the way, what are you doing after lunch?'

She was asking Charlotte, but she meant Saul, who was sitting back and looking, Charlotte had to admit, the most impressive man in the room for anybody's money. 'Looking at a house,' said Charlotte.

'Oho?' Jo-Ann's voice rose. 'You mean——?' She waggled her finger, linking them, and Charlotte said raggedly, 'Not for us, for heaven's sake,' and then bit her lip and felt herself flushing.

Saul said, 'For me. Charlotte is giving me the benefit of a little friendly advice.'

'That's nice,' said Jo-Ann. 'You're coming to live down here?'

'Probably.'

'Very nice,' said Jo-Ann, and turned to Charlotte to ask, 'How's Jeremy these days?'

'Oh, just fine,' said Charlotte.

'You're still seeing him?'

'Of course.'

'I wondered if you'd split.'

'No danger,' said Charlotte, resisting the temptation to say, 'And no business of yours if we had.'

'Well, goodbye for now, then,' said Jo-Ann. 'See you again some time.' She smiled at Saul, and managed to make that sound full of promise, and Saul said, 'I hope so.'

When Jo-Ann was safely back at her table he asked, 'Do you have many friends like her?'

'Not many.' Jo-Ann had never really been a friend, more of a rival even at school. It would have boosted her ego to take a man away from Charlotte, and if Charlotte had had any designs on Saul herself she would have been keeping an eye on Jo-Ann. She said tartly, 'I'm pretty sure you'll get an invitation to a dinner party in the next week or two.'

'Shall I?' said Saul, with the uninterest of a man who need never spend an evening alone. Then he grinned. 'Well, it's nice to know that some of the natives are friendly.'

'I'm sure we all are,' said Charlotte, but she knew that he felt the hostility too. Even when they were smiling at each other it was just below the surface. Jo-Ann was a man-eater, but she would find this one too tough to handle, and Charlotte would feel almost sorry for her if she tried.

She was still at her table when they left the dining room, and she waved vivaciously at them, and the two aunts in their summer straw hats craned their necks to see . . .

Saul didn't tell Charlotte to put on her seat-belt this time, and having made an issue of refusal she couldn't very well change her mind. They went across country to the last house, saving several miles by cutting through the lanes. Charlotte directed, the wine making her feel relaxed even with Saul beside her. She watched his hands on the wheel and thought, He drives like an expert. I wonder if he can handle a horse. I wonder how he would handle a woman.

Not, of course, that she was interested in his sensual expertise, but seeing Jo-Ann ogling him had made her realise that to some women he might seem a disturbingly sexy man. 'It's hot in here,' she said, running a finger round the neck of her shirt. 'Can I turn up the cold air?'

The windows were open but she was hot, and the sun was bright on the windscreen so that she hardly saw the other car. It came straight across the crossroads, although this was the major road, and Saul had to slam on his brakes to avoid ploughing into it. At the same time he flung an arm across Charlotte or she would have gone head-first through the windscreen. As it was, she hit the glass with her forehead with a force that knocked her unconscious.

The terror only lasted a moment before the impact, but it was long enough for her to taste death, and her mouth seemed full of bitter acid when she opened her eyes and Saul's face swam over her. He had an arm around her. Behind him, through the open window, was a red face with shocked bulging eyes, topped by a checked cap.

'It's all right,' said Saul, and miraculously it was. Her ears were ringing like a peal of discordant bells, and her head felt numb, as though it was stuffed with cotton wool. But she knew how narrow her escape had been and that he had saved her from being slashed to ribbons.

The headache would come later, but right now all that mattered was that she was alive, she was all right, she was so lucky. She tried to lift her head, but everything went spinning and she heard Saul say, 'We're getting you to hospital . . .'

'Yes, I remember,' she said, some fifteen minutes later. 'A car came out and we had to brake. I suppose the driver was the man in the flat cap. He's a menace on the road.'

'The roads are full of menaces,' sighed the emergency doctor, who saw the results of many of them. A nursing Sister checked Charlotte's blood pressure and pulse rate. The doctor had examined her eyes' reaction to light, and now he wanted to know whether there was any loss of memory leading up to her slamming her head against the windscreen. There wasn't, and that seemed to be a good sign, but even after the X-rays had shown no fracture it was no guarantee against bruising of the brain.

Actually she wasn't told that. Saul was. The Sister was repeating the doctor's instructions, that Charlotte had had a nasty thump and should go to bed for twenty-four hours, and mustn't take anything stronger than a couple of Paracetemols because if the headache got really bad they would want to know. The doctor was talking to Saul, and Charlotte was listening to what he had to say, although she was nodding at the Sister.

In the car she said, 'Bruising of the brain sounds terrible. What else did he say that I couldn't hear?'

'Things to watch out for,' said Saul.

'Such as?'

'Severe vomiting. Disorientation.'

'Fantastic,' she said. 'I'll look forward to that.' A bump of sizeable proportions throbbed on the hairline of her forehead and she wanted to get home to Aunt Lucy. It was a long time since she had run to Aunt Lucy with a cut knee or a bee sting, but right now it seemed like yesterday and she felt like a small girl again with a tear-stained face.

In fact her cheeks were dry and she put on a brave face, and when the car drew up at home she opened the car door and waved across at old Tom, who was weeding, with a long-handled hoe because he couldn't manage the bending any more. But suddenly she wasn't sure that her legs would support her. Now she was home and safe the shock was telling, and she bit her lip and asked Saul, 'Would you fetch Aunt Lucy, please? I'm not disorientating, I'm just feeling slightly the worse for wear.'

'Sure,' he said. He went into the house and Charlotte sat waiting. When he came out he was alone, and he went across to Tom and spoke to him, then came to Charlotte and said, 'Miss Snowe's not in at the moment.'

'Where is she?'

'Gone into Stratford.' And it wasn't Maudie's day, so there was nobody at home, and she would have to get herself to bed, so she had better get on her feet. 'Come on,' said Saul.

'I *can* walk.' But the headache was starting. She prayed, please God, don't let it get too bad, and Saul said, 'Take it easy, they said,' and picked her up as though she was still a child.

She didn't want *that*. She wouldn't have minded a helping hand, but she didn't want holding so that her cheek was pressed against his chest and her arms were round his neck. That seemed the only place for her arms to go, and she didn't have the strength to argue or struggle, although when he started to carry her upstairs she did say, 'I could lie down on the sofa.'

'Not for the next twenty-four hours,' he said. 'You'll be better in bed. Which is your room?'

'Second floor.' She reached to turn the knob, babbling, 'I'll wear a seat-belt after this. I don't feel bad at all really, but I think I'll have those two headache pills if you'd just get them for me from the bathroom cupboard. I'll just kick my shoes off and——'

'You'll just shut up,' he said. He set her down on the edge of the bed, seated, and took off her sandals, and she thought it would have been nice if he had rubbed her bare feet for a while because her toes were twitching with nerves. But when she realised he was undoing the little buttons of her shirt she stiffened, protesting, 'I can manage.'

'Good,' he grinned, and somehow it was a nice grin that took the tension out of her. 'But remember there isn't much of you that I haven't seen.'

'There's enough,' she heard herself giggle weakly.

'Then I'll find your pills.'

While he was gone Charlotte got out of her clothes and into a nightdress and crawled between the sheets. She would take the pills and rest and know soon enough if there was any damage done. At the moment she couldn't be sure she was all right, the bump was throbbing away.

She might feel better after resting or she might feel worse, and she wished Aunt Lucy were here to sit by her bed.

Saul brought the pills and water and she swallowed, then lay back on the pillow, and he leaned over her and for a moment she thought he was going to kiss her. That would have been comforting. When he didn't she faltered, 'What is it?'

'Not a thing,' he said. 'You're fine.'

'Then why were you looking at me like that?'

'Would you believe to check if your pupils match? They do, both the same size, and that means you're fine.'

She looked up into his eyes and felt his breath on her parted lips like the lightest of kisses, and said, 'Will you stay until somebody comes?'

'Of course,' he said, and Charlotte closed her eyes and let herself drift into sleep, and she wasn't afraid any more because Saul was staying with her and with him she was safe.

CHAPTER FOUR

CHARLOTTE woke at Aunt Lucy's touch and blinked at the fear in her big moon face. 'Oh, my poor lamb,' Aunt Lucy was whispering. 'What happened to you?'

Then Charlotte remembered, and touched the bump on her forehead and winced. Her head was aching, but not unbearably, and she was feeling sick but not to the stage of severe vomiting. What was the other thing? Disorientation. Well, the room seemed to be steady enough, and so did dear old Aunt Lucy, who was such a picture of misery that Charlotte said quickly, 'Nothing to what could have happened—I was very lucky.'

'I wouldn't call this being lucky!' Reassured, Aunt Lucy was turning querulous. 'Not a scratch on Mr Laurenson, I notice. It's only you who nearly goes through the wind-screen.'

She sounded in a mood to accuse Saul of reckless driving at least, and Charlotte said, 'If it hadn't been for Saul I would have gone through the window. I wasn't wearing a seat-belt and he held me back, and the accident wasn't his fault, because this idiot cut straight out in front of us.'

'Oh,' said Aunt Lucy. 'Well, in that case I'm sorry I was sharp with him.'

She was still wearing her coat and hat and she must have just returned from her shopping. As soon as Saul broke the news that Charlotte was in bed, as the result of a car accident, Aunt Lucy would be up here as fast as her bulk would let her. Charlotte wondered what she had said to Saul, who had surely had enough trouble for one afternoon. Not, she thought, that Saul would be cut to the quick by Aunt Lucy.

She was feeling better. Her face had been wiped clean at the hospital, but Aunt Lucy, with an inborn instinct for coddling, said, 'I'll just sponge your hands and face,' and brought a basin and a cloth and gently dabbed away, finishing with an eau-de-cologne soaked handkerchief tucked under Charlotte's pillow. 'Now,' she said, 'do you fancy a cup of tea?'

That was welcome. Charlotte sat up and sipped, and explained that she didn't need any food because she had had an outsize lunch. It was nearly five o'clock now, and she must have slept for a good two hours, although she wouldn't have put it that long. Georgy had come into the room some time and was curled on his rug viewing Aunt Lucy's comings and goings with some surprise, and after her cup of tea Charlotte said, 'I should think I could get up.'

'Not till the doctor's seen you,' said Aunt Lucy firmly.

'I've seen a doctor. I went to the hospital and it's only a little bump.'

Aunt Lucy whipped up a silver-backed mirror from the dressing table and handed it over without a word, and Charlotte gasped at her reflection. This was no little bump. This was a great shining swelling, with the dark beginnings of an ugly bruise. The skin was unbroken, but it was visible proof of the force with which she had hit that windscreen, and it silenced her about jumping out of bed.

'Mr Laurenson phoned Dr Buckston,' Aunt Lucy fussed around, smoothing the counterpane. 'He was out, but he'll be along, and what your father's going to say about this I do not know.'

'Warn him it looks worse than it is,' said Charlotte. 'I must have a thick skull, because I had an X-ray and there's nothing cracked.' Aunt Lucy tutted, with her such-

goings-on expression. 'What did you say to Saul?'
Charlotte enquired.

'I asked him what he'd been doing to you.'

'Treating me very gently, actually, all things considering,' said Charlotte wryly.

When Aunt Lucy had left her she lay thinking how
strange it was that Saul should seem protective and kind
when she was hurt and vulnerable, and yet when she was
strong and sound in mind and body he seemed almost
wholly threatening. Of course it would take a callous man
not to be concerned when his passenger took a nosedive
at the windscreen, but the memory of his touch lingered
on her skin. She recalled his fingers undoing the buttons
of her shirt, and she was breathing fast, and she wondered
how it would have been if he had kissed her, if his hand
had covered a breast.

Georgy's huge eyes were fixed on her and she said,
'Can't you figure out what's going on? Well, neither can
I, so maybe this is the beginning of that disorientation.'
She laughed at herself then and thought, So he's sexy,
and he carried me up here and practically put me to bed,
and I'm only human. It wouldn't be hard to fancy him,
but that doesn't mean to say I like him. Jeremy is the
man I like, the man I love and trust. Next time anyone
looked in she would ask for a phone, because she must
ring Jeremy and tell him what had happened to her.

She woke to a yelp from Georgy as Dr Buckston
advanced on the bed. The doctor was an old family friend,
but that didn't stop Georgy from backing under the
dressing table and going on yapping until her father
dragged him out and handed him over to Aunt Lucy.
'And what have you been up to, young Charlotte?' asked
Dr Buckston.

Her father looked worried; she always seemed to be
worrying him lately. 'It could have been worse,' she said,

'I don't know how we missed crashing into that other car.' She remembered Saul swerving to avoid Kelly and said, 'He's getting a lot of practice dodging things these days,' then grimaced when the two men looked puzzled. 'Sorry, just a little private joke.'

Dr Buckston checked her pulse and blood pressure again, shone a torch into her eyes, and finally smiled, agreeing that it could have been worse. She must stay where she was until tomorrow evening, but she was a very fortunate young lady, escaping with a bump and a bruise.

He didn't say, 'Instead of a lacerated face and possibly a cut throat,' but that was what he was thinking, and so was her father. Her father was looking haggard, and Charlotte reached across impulsively to take his hand and say to the doctor, 'While you're here, this is the one you should be examining. He's beginning to look very tired. Can't you give him a tonic?'

'He knows the tonic I recommend.' William Buckston looked over his spectacles at his friend. 'More leisure and less work.'

Her father had never been a dynamic business man, theirs wasn't that kind of business, but if the doctor thought he had too much on his shoulders Charlotte could take on more responsibility for the day-to-day running of Dunscombes. She said, 'Maybe it's time we made it Dunscombe and Daughter,' and her father chuckled and she thought, He's like Aunt Lucy, he still thinks I'm a child.

'Don't worry,' he said, 'I'm hoping to take things easier before long.'

'Well, it can't be too soon,' said Dr Buckston. 'And how about a round of golf next week?'

It had to be a good idea that she should lie here, as two doctors had given the orders, but having slept most of the afternoon and into early evening Charlotte lay wakeful and bored from about eight o'clock. She had spoken to Jeremy earlier.

'Hello, love,' he'd said, 'I got your message. Are you coming round later?'

'Not today,' she said. 'I was in a near-miss car accident and now I'm lying in bed, nursing a bump on my forehead, and they won't let me get up till tomorrow morning.'

Jeremy's concern was gratifying. She could feel it coming over the phone in comforting waves, lapping her in love. He was appalled to think that Charlotte had been close to a real catastrophe. Was she sure she was all right? Did it hurt still? How had it happened?

She told him how it had happened, with Saul Laurenson at the wheel, and Jeremy exclaimed, 'I'll kill him—risking your neck! He should have seen the other car.'

'There were high hedges,' she explained, but that wasn't good enough for Jeremy.

'There were crossroads, weren't there? He should have slowed down.'

'If you slowed down at every hidden gate or road going along the lanes when you'd got right of way,' Charlotte pointed out, 'you'd never get anywhere.'

'What were you doing in his car anyway?'

'He's looking at houses round here. My father lined me up to go with him.'

'Why?'

'I like looking at houses, usually, and I'm local, of course.' She began to smile. 'You wouldn't be jealous, would you?'

'Not so long as you still think he looks like Dracula,' said Jeremy.

'Oh, he does.' Dracula carrying her upstairs, leaning

over her as she lay on the bed, dynamic and dark and very sexy. She was glad that Jeremy couldn't read her thoughts, and she said, 'I wish you could come over. You can't, though, my father's in no mood for letting you into my bedroom. I'll be up tomorrow, I'll see you the next day.'

'And it is only a bruise you've got, and no complications and nothing else?'

'Would I lie to you?' She laughed, cradling the receiver. 'Really, that's all.'

'That's a clever girl.' Jeremy breathed deep. 'Bloody mad drivers, not knowing what they're doing half the time!' She supposed he meant Saul, as well as the man in the flat cap, and she thought, He knows what he's doing. He was never out of control of that car, he was always in control of everything.

She said, 'Goodbye for now. Give the audience something to remember—and I wish I could be watching you from the wings.'

Her father had brought in a portable TV and Charlotte watched that for a while. She was into a play that promised to be entertaining when Aunt Lucy came back again with the phone and announced, 'It's that Jo-Ann Marley.' Aunt Lucy had never had much room for Jo-Ann since Charlotte's sixth birthday party when Jo-Ann had asked her, 'Why does Charlotte call you Aunt Lucy? You're not her auntie, are you. You're only a servant, aren't you?'

She had told Jo-Ann that Charlotte was resting, and why, and Jo-Ann had sounded very shocked and asked if it would be possible to have a word with her, so Aunt Lucy had relented and brought up the phone.

'Why, hello,' said Charlotte, with no illusions at all as to why Jo-Ann was ringing. She wanted the lowdown on Saul, and although she was sorry about Charlotte's crack on the head, as soon as Charlotte had said she'd live Jo-Ann asked, 'Was Saul with you?'

'Yes.'

'He's all right, is he?' Now that *would* have been a tragedy, thought Charlotte. Girls Jo-Ann could do without, but she would have suffered at the loss of an eligible man. She said,

'Not a mark on him. At least, none he showed me.'

'Good,' said Jo-Ann. 'I say, who *is* he?'

'A friend of my father's.'

'Not yours?'

'Not particularly.' More like an enemy. All the warning signals in her blood were ringing for him, and she frowned and went to rub her forehead and touched the bruise and cowered.

Jo-Ann asked, 'Is he married?'

'No,' said Charlotte. She added sarcastically, 'Not married and rich and probably coming to live round here, so isn't that exciting?' But Jo-Ann was thick-skinned as they come and agreed enthusiastically, then went on,

'Is he at your place now?'

Charlotte had asked her father that, and been told that Saul had gone back to his hotel, and now she said, 'No, he's staying at the Blue Boar.'

'Well, hurry up and get well,' said Jo-Ann, and rang off, hardly giving Charlotte time to say goodbye.

Charlotte banged down the phone and let out her breath in a long exasperated gasp, then sagged, deflated, against the pillows. Jo-Ann would phone him all right and maybe he should be warned, and Charlotte threw back the sheets, on her way to look up the number of the Blue Boar in the directory downstairs.

Then she checked herself. She wasn't responsible for what Jo-Ann did, and if ever a man could look after himself Saul Laurenson could. Besides she was still feeling groggy. She lay down again and tried to watch the play, but from then on it seemed to get sillier, until the whole thing was bogged down in talk-talk-talk and she turned it off.

She couldn't relax. Even her favourite books, that she kept in a bookcase in her room, failed to soothe her, and when Aunt Lucy looked in she kept her talking until Aunt Lucy protested, 'You're supposed to be resting, not chattering nineteen to the dozen.'

'I'm not tired. I'm getting up in the morning.'

'Are you, my lady? We'll see about that. Anyhow, what's happening tomorrow that makes it so important for you to be up and about?'

'Nothing that I know of,' said Charlotte. But things were happening, all connected with Saul Laurenson, and it would be stupid to stay in bed when, after a night's sleep, she would be perfectly fine.

She could have slept better. Aunt Lucy brought her another couple of pills with a glass of hot milk before she settled down, but she did a lot of dreaming and tossing that night. They were dreams she couldn't remember, but she woke from them several times and lay staring into the darkness and she couldn't get the dark face of Saul Laurenson out of her mind . . .

'Cup of tea?' said Aunt Lucy, and Charlotte opened her eyes and sat up and smiled. Her headache was now no more than a niggle, and there were no other aches and pains. 'No damage,' she said, with heartfelt relief because until now she hadn't been quite sure that her injuries were superficial.

'That's a beautiful bruise,' commented Aunt Lucy.

'I'll comb a fringe over it. What's the time?'

'Seven o'clock. You drink your tea and go back to sleep.'

'Yes, I will.' Charlotte could do that today, without

feeling guilty about Aunt Lucy being up and about. Today she was convalescent, until after nine o'clock anyway, when her father should have left the house and she would only have Aunt Lucy to contend with.

Her father came into her room around eight o'clock, dressing gown over pyjamas and grey-faced as though he hadn't slept too well, and Charlotte gave him a specially bright and reassuring smile.

'Lucy says you're feeling better.' He stood beside her bed, frowning at the purple swelling on her forehead.

'I'm feeling fine.' She squinted at the bump, which was big enough to see with her eyes crossed. 'Better out than in.' She started to laugh, then sobered. 'Saul held me back, you know. He threw an arm across me while he was braking. If he hadn't——' She bit her lip and wished she had not brought up what would have happened if Saul's reflexes had been slower. She said wryly, 'I don't know about my life, but I guess I owe him my face.'

'Don't forget that,' her father said. 'And you stay where you are until I get back this evening, then you can come downstairs.' He kissed her cheek and told her, 'I love you.'

It was a long time since he had told her that, and she supposed it was because of the accident, because he might have lost her. 'Whatever happens,' he said, 'remember I love you.'

So he was speaking for the future. But while she was asking, 'What do you mean——?' he was walking away, and when he looked in again he was dressed for work and just off.

'And this is where I expect to find you when I come back,' he told her. 'Don't get being too clever.'

'I'm not feeling *too* clever,' she had to admit. Even a slight headache was a handicap. She would need all her wits to deal with whatever was going on around here, but by evening she would be back in fighting form.

She had no doubt there was a fight looming. She had never had to fight anyone before, let alone a man like Saul Laurenson. You only had to look at him to know he was a winner who didn't believe in rules, so she was forearmed there; but he could have a surprise. She looked soft and sweet and pampered, but she was almost sure she had a core of toughness. 'Wait for it,' she told herself, telling him although he couldn't hear her, 'because I don't trust you and I don't fancy being a loser either.'

The headache got better. By the time the roses arrived it had gone, and Charlotte, who had read the newspapers from beginning to end and eaten a small tuna salad for her lunch, was bored.

Aunt Lucy brought up the bouquet, dark red and fragrant, and Charlotte bounced up in bed with delight. 'Oh, how gorgeous, are they for me?'

'Nobody sends me roses,' said Aunt Lucy.

'Who are they from?'

Aunt Lucy put them on the bed and Charlotte read the little card, 'For a clever girl, love, J.' That was thoughtful of Jeremy. She had told him not to come, but this was a lovely idea, and she brushed one of the velvety petals with her lips. 'Do you want them up here?' asked Aunt Lucy.

Charlotte wasn't staying up here. She was going downstairs and she wanted her roses with her. She got out of bed, her roses in her arms. 'And where do you think you're going?' Aunt Lucy demanded.

'To put them in water. Then I'm getting up.' She wheedled, 'Oh, come on, I can't lie in bed any longer. I'll come down and sit on the sofa. I'm not going to have a relapse now, am I?'

'The doctor said you were to stay in bed till teatime. So did your father.'

'We won't tell them,' said Charlotte.

Aunt Lucy hesitated, but, apart from the bruise, Charlotte looked her usual healthy self, and the stairs were steep and Lucy Snowe felt she could watch over her just as well in the drawing room. 'All right,' she said grudgingly. 'Give them here.'

Charlotte put on a red velvet robe that matched the roses, tied with a broad girdle that emphasised her slender waist. She wondered if Jeremy might turn up. If he did they might not let him come upstairs to see her, but they could hardly keep him out of the drawing room and the robe was a complement to the roses.

They looked very effective in a big white bowl on a low table, and Charlotte, sitting on her heels, fiddled around until they were arranged to her satisfaction.

The phone rang a couple of times. She had heard it ringing earlier while she was in bed, when Aunt Lucy or Maudie had answered. The news of her escapade was going the rounds and friends were phoning. Down here she answered, and told a couple of friends that the man in the car with her was a business colleague of her father's. Nothing to do with her. He might be buying a house and she was just looking with him. She didn't want any of them linking her with Saul Laurenson, because no way were she and he likely to get together.

A third call was Jo-Ann Marley, and Charlotte wished she hadn't taken that, because she didn't have much to say to Jo-Ann.

Yes, thank you, she said, she was much better today. It had really been next to nothing anyway, but it was nice of Jo-Ann to be asking. Only that wasn't why Jo-Ann was calling, so Charlotte waited and after a moment or two Jo-Ann said, 'By the way, I saw Saul last night.'

'Did you?'

Jo-Ann was getting confidential. Her voice sounded as though she was smiling a smug little smile. 'Well, I rang him—well, you'd said he wasn't a particular friend, and anyway, it's you and Jeremy Wylde, isn't it? or of course I wouldn't have.' The heck you wouldn't! thought Charlotte. 'He asked me to have dinner with him,' said Jo-Ann.

'Quick work,' said Charlotte. She was surprised. She wouldn't have thought Jo-Ann was Saul Laurenson's type, although of course she was a very pretty girl and goodness knows she was available. 'Have a nice time?' she asked, and Jo-Ann gurgled,

'You can say that again! I really did.' She sounded as if she was hugging herself. 'He's fan*tas*tic, and so hand-some.'

'Do you think so?' said Charlotte. 'I think he looks like Dracula,' and Jo-Ann went into squeals of laugh-ter,

'Well, he can take a bite out of me any time!'

'Ha ha,' said Charlotte. 'Oh, hello, how nice to see you. Sorry, Jo-Ann, I'll have to ring off, I've got a visitor.' There was nobody in the room but the dogs, and there was nobody coming, but she couldn't stand Jo-Ann a moment longer. The girl was a *fool*, flirting with any man in sight. Charlotte could just imagine her, simpering across the dinner table at Saul; and if she knew Jo-Ann the evening's entertainment wouldn't end with dinner.

Perhaps they ate in his suite. Charlotte could imagine that scene: the round table, perhaps candlelight, and two chairs drawn up; the half-open door into the other room, which would be in shadowy darkness. And she was filled with a violent impatience, frustration, anger almost. An emotion that she couldn't give a name but that could not possibly be jealousy.

Her head was starting to throb again, warning her that she must take things calmly, that bump was a weak spot for a while; so she lay down on the big soft-cushioned

Chesterfield, and closed her eyes and waited for the throbbing to subside.

She heard the doorbell ring and the dogs rushed out of the room, Georgy well behind Wilbur and Tria. Then there was barking and somebody being let in, and she thought, it's going to be Jeremy, so she stayed where she was, lying back and doing her best to look pale and interesting.

But it was Saul, and she wasn't surprised. Day and night lately she never seemed to be free of him. She sat up and he asked, 'How are you feeling?'

'Oh,' she shrugged, 'all right. No delayed action with you?'

'Nothing happened to me yesterday.'

Charlotte said tartly, before she could stop herself, 'I wouldn't say that.' She hadn't meant to say anything and she babbled on, 'It was a pretty near thing, it could have shaken anybody. You might have felt some sort of shock later.' But he had nerves of steel, she was sure of it, so she stopped pretending she had been referring to the accident and asked, 'Was it a pleasant evening with Jo-Ann?'

'Very.'

'She phoned me twice—once to find out where you were and once to tell me she'd seen you.' Now she was sounding amused, asking, 'What did she say? "Hello and are you at a loose end tonight?" or "How about a drink to celebrate your escape? You must be a fantastic driver." ' She drawled the 'fantastic' in a way that Jo-Ann had, and he laughed.

'You're not too far off, but it started with an offer to help me find a house. She tells me she was in real estate for a while.'

'She was in an estate office,' Charlotte recalled. 'For a few weeks a few years ago.' Jo-Ann had gone from job to job when she first left school, her looks and confidence impressing the interviewers and opening the doors. But as jobs became scarce that stopped, and now she was a student again, taking an art course and always on the watch for a man. Jo-Ann intended to marry well, and although Charlotte did not imagine for a moment that Saul Laurenson would get that involved she wished she could warn him. She said slowly, 'She's very attractive, but she's not one of my best friends.'

'That's funny.' Saul had seated himself and was scratching the top of Georgy's head. Georgy was very still. 'Because she said you were her very dearest friend.' Something unpleasant was coming, Charlotte knew, before he added gravely, 'Mind you, she did say you'd never done a day's work in your life and men made such fools of themselves over you.'

Charlotte began to splutter furiously, then she began to laugh because, coming from Jo-Ann, that *was* funny. Charlotte worked a darn sight harder than she did and some men had behaved ridiculously over Charlotte, but she had never exploited them, while Jo-Ann would have taken their last penny before she waved goodbye.

'The nerve of the girl!' Charlotte grinned. 'And all I was going to do was warn you that she's a cow.' Then it struck her that he might imagine she was trying to put him off Jo-Ann because she was interested in him herself, playing an identical game to Jo-Ann, in short, and she said hastily, 'There are some super girls round here that I could introduce you to.'

'No, thanks.' He was sitting by the bowl of roses and he leaned across to read the card. 'For a clever girl.' His dark brows rose. 'Is that you?'

'Yes.'

'You did nothing clever. All you did was nearly get yourself killed.'

She knew that. Anyhow, those words didn't matter. 'Love, J,' was what mattered, red roses for love. If Jeremy had been here now he would be sitting beside her, comforting her. She wondered if Saul had put his arms around Jo-Ann last night, and felt suddenly empty and lonely. She said stiffly, 'I have to thank you—if you hadn't held me back I would have been badly cut, perhaps worse. Actually I am into the habit of wearing a seat-belt, but when you ordered me to put it on that put my back up. I hate being bossed about.'

He said quietly, 'That's another habit you might have to get into,' and she wondered if she had heard aright. If she had she knew who the boss would be, and it was hard to look unflinchingly at him and ask,

'Would you care to explain that?'

'Your father should be here any minute.' He smiled with unsmiling eyes. 'Perhaps it's time we had a get-together of the interested parties.'

Charlotte was supposed to be upstairs still, in bed. When her father arrived he wouldn't expect to find her here, but nothing could have dragged her away now. 'High time,' she said, 'if you have plans that include giving me your orders. But until my father gets here would you mind waiting in another room? I still have a headache.'

Saul said, 'Of course,' and that perhaps she should carry on resting, but she retorted, 'Some hope, after what you've just said!' She wanted him to go quickly before she started to panic and bombard him with questions, but as he reached the door she asked, 'Is anything I might have to say likely to make any difference?'

'No,' he said, and she knew that everything was signed and sealed. He stood in the doorway, head turned, looking at her for what seemed a very long time, and her tongue stuck to the roof of her mouth so that she couldn't speak until he had closed the door after him, then the words came out in a whisper: 'What do you want from *me*?'

Dunscombes was the family firm and of course what

happened to it mattered to her, and would matter to everybody working there. But just now, when Saul Laurenson looked at her, it had seemed more personal than that. Something between the two of them, something he wanted from her. She felt as trapped as though he had caught her wrist in his strong fingers and pulled her towards him, and she picked up Georgy and hugged him, burying her face in the warm talcum-scented fur. 'Why did you sit there and let him stroke you?' she demanded. 'Paralysed with fright, probably, and well you might be!'

Her robe was only secured by the belt. If it fell open her only covering would be a thin nightdress, and she wondered whether she should go up to her room and dress. But if her father was due any minute she would like to get that 'get-together of the interested parties' over first. She might be needing to take a walk after that, if it was only down to the bottom of the garden to sit in the cool air of the patio. She would ring Jeremy and ask him to meet her. She might be needing Jeremy.

She took one of the shorter-stemmed roses from the bowl, then opened drawers in a black ebony Chinese bureau until she found a safety pin, and pinned the rose at her throat fastening the robe. That covered her securely. She was anxious to be covered.

She tried to get Jeremy, but there was no answer, either from his flat or the theatre. She was still listening to the ringing, in what must be an empty theatre, when she heard her father's car and put down the receiver. She wished somebody had answered, it would have made her feel less alone. She was safe at home, with Aunt Lucy within earshot and her father coming into the house, but as she stood there she felt a terrifying isolation.

Her father and Saul Laurenson came into the room together. Her father was shaking his head at her, going on about her getting up before she should have done, exclaiming at the blue-black colour of her bruised forehead. But she couldn't take her eyes off Saul Laurenson.

'Sit down,' ordered her father. 'You know you should still be resting.'

She sat and so did he, but Saul walked towards the fireplace and stood there, facing them as though he was host here, and Charlotte said, 'I'm all right. All I want to know is—what's going on?'

'You mean about the business?' Her father spoke very slowly and deliberately, but her words came in a rush because the time for hedging was over.

'Yes, that is what I mean. If we do still have a business. I suppose Dunscombes hasn't become Laurensons?'

'Not quite,' said her father ruefully, 'but perhaps it should, because it's a long time since Dunscombes made a healthy profit.'

He had never told her that until yesterday, and she said now, 'Well, who does make a healthy profit these days?'

'I do,' said Saul.

'And what do you do for it?' She resented his success when her father had the look of a beaten man. 'Who are you anyway?' she demanded harshly, and her father made a protesting gesture, hushing her, telling her,

'Among other things Saul owns shops and department stores, here and abroad. He has the selling outlets, the export markets.'

'Well, well,' she drawled, 'a real-life tycoon! And what are your plans for us?' She knew that times were changing, but individually crafted items couldn't be turned out in vast quantities by their small staff, so what was the use of talking about department stores and exports?

Her father was talking about reorganisation now and she asked, 'Must we?'

'The alternative is to close down,' he said simply, and she went cold.

'That bad?'

He nodded, and Charlotte couldn't believe that she hadn't known. But there had been no redundancies, nothing to show they were no longer a flourishing firm. 'So what's going to happen?' she asked, and she looked at Saul and thought, It was right, what I feared, he's the take-over man.

Her father said, 'No one will lose their job, that's part of the agreement.'

'How about you?' Dunscombes had been his life. He had managed the business as well as owning it.

'I shall carry on,' he said, 'but without the responsibility, and I can do without that.'

Taking orders, in short. Working for Saul Laurenson. She asked, 'And what about me?'

Saul spoke for the first time in a long time. All the while he had been watching them, and when he spoke she clutched her robe tighter around her, almost crushing the rose before she realised what she was doing. 'I was impressed by some of your designs,' he told her. 'I'm sure we can keep you occupied.'

'That is kind of you. Shall I need the work?' She made herself smile, and her father said, 'You've always enjoyed it, haven't you? Always had a flair.'

'Yes', she agreed, 'I enjoy it.' He hadn't said she need not work for the new management, and she wanted to ask, 'What kind of deal is this? How much is he paying and what's left?' but she felt as though the ground was shifting beneath her feet.

Her father looked grey, his face and his hair. She wanted to kneel beside him and put her arms around him and tell him it was going to be all right, but she could do none of that in front of Saul Laurenson.

She said, 'Well, it's a shock. A bombshell. I just didn't have a clue that all this was going on and I think I've heard as much as I can take in for a while. I'll go up to my room now, I think, and I'll see you later.' She smiled again, stretching her lips, and stooped to pick up Georgy, holding him so tightly that he wriggled.

Upstairs she waited for her father to come. She had dressed, putting on the first thing that she took out of the wardrobe. It was a lightweight linen dress, but if it had been thick wool she would still have got into it, because her mind wasn't on what she was doing.

Georgy sensed trouble and watched her with the whites of his eyes showing and his ears twitching. When her father came into the room she ran across to him, and he put his arms around her and said, 'It's going to be all right.'

That was what she had been going to tell him, she felt he was more in need of comfort than she was, and she said now, 'Yes, of course, I know that, but tell me—does he own the business? Do we have any say in anything any more?'

'Sit down.' She sat on the edge of the bed and her father crossed to the window, talking with his back to her as though he couldn't face her. 'You know, don't you, that you matter more to me than anything else in the world?'

'Yes, of course. So do you to me, and if you've had to sell out I understand that. I only wish you'd told me sooner so that I could have helped. Done something, maybe.'

'There's something you can do,' he told her, and she had almost reached him, to kiss him and promise him anything, when he said the words that stopped her dead. 'You can marry Saul.'

CHAPTER FIVE

'WHAT?' exclaimed Charlotte. '*What?*' Her father didn't repeat his words, he knew she had heard him. He didn't turn either and she stood looking at his back as he stared unseeingly out of the window. The stooped shoulders didn't look like her father, who had always been straight and upright and strong. Then he said,

'We're in a bad way. If Saul hadn't taken over the business I don't know what we should have done.'

'I've never heard of him.' He owned Dunscombes and until three days ago she had never heard his name.

'He left England fifteen years ago. He used to have a stall on Wickham market.' That was one of the smaller local markets, and Charlotte said,

'Small beginnings. Or did he have shops there too?'

'Just the one stall—selling saddlery, that sort of thing. He was seventeen. Two years later he had stalls in half a dozen markets. Then he went to Australia.'

'And he's come back a millionaire?'

'At least.'

'He did well.'

'Yes.' Colin Dunscombe straightened and his voice strengthened, and she knew that he was pulling himself together before he turned to face her. 'He hasn't changed much. I knew him at once when I saw him again.'

'Did he always look like Dracula?' Charlotte asked idiotically, and her father stared at her, puzzled, then smiled.

'He always had a lean and hungry look. He always stood out as someone who would outpace the rest. I met him in Antwerp in February.' Antwerp was the diamond centre where her father, as a manufacturing jeweller, went to buy uncut stones. 'We nearly passed each other just outside the Rubens house. He asked me to have dinner with him that night and we talked. He was there because he owned the hotel we were eating in, and I was there because it was the time of year I always went to Antwerp. I wasn't buying anything. I was wondering where I could start looking for a buyer for Dunscombes.'

'You should have told me.' He had brought her back a present. He had never said anything about business worries, and now he asked,

'What good would it have done? I didn't want you worrying. Saul was the first man I told.'

'You can trust him?'

'Oh yes.' He sounded confident, and it was too late for her to point out that self-made millionaires usually worked for their own interests. Right now she didn't care much about that. What did make her heart ache was the fact that her father hadn't confided in her, that he had kept all this to himself until he met a man he hadn't seen in fifteen years. Where were his friends? He had so many friends. Some, like accountants and bank managers, were there to advise on business matters. Why couldn't he have turned to someone close at hand rather than a stranger, met by chance in a foreign land?

'You'll be all right now,' he said, and he was smiling. 'It's all working out very well.'

'Is it?'

'Saul thinks it's time he settled down, that he's been a bachelor long enough.' He said this with a twinkle in his eye, as though it was something Charlotte should find interesting. 'I showed him your photograph. He said you were very beautiful, that I must be very proud of you. I think he was half in love with you before he even saw you.'

'Oh no,' she said. She believed her father had shown Saul Laurenson her photograph, probably that first evening when they were dining together and he was pouring out the troubles he had kept to himself till then. And she was photogenic and Saul had said what any man would say to a proud father, but even if he had admired her photograph he hadn't been impressed after he set eyes on her. As for falling in love, with a photograph or a woman, what her father meant by that and what Saul Laurenson would mean were poles apart.

He must be thirty-four now. Perhaps he did feel it was time he was looking around for a wife. He could afford to buy the best, and her stomach clenched with nausea. It was like a slave auction, a cattle market. Was that why her father had been so prejudiced against Jeremy, because he was hoping she would land Saul Laurenson, millionaire at least? Had Saul come here to look her over?

She felt a chill in her bones and said, 'I hope you didn't tell him I'm looking for a husband?'

'Of course not!'

Oh, Jeremy, she thought, Jeremy; and her voice caught in her throat. 'Because when I do I won't be after a tycoon who's decided to go shopping for a wife. That sort would be trading you in for a later model in a few years' time.'

Her father winced, and she knew that he had hoped she would fall in love and that Saul Laurenson would love her. To her father she was the perfect wife for the man who had everything else, and she grinned wryly, 'I'm not that great a bargain, you know, he must know lots of better-looking girls, and between the two of us he's not very taken with me.'

Saul Laurenson didn't want her any more than she wanted him, but her father was distressed enough without having to face another scene, and she said, 'Forget it. Maybe I'll go for a ride.'

'You won't. You're supposed to be resting for twenty-four hours. You could have concussion.'

She had forgotten that. Her head was whirling, but well it might. She said, 'All right, I'll lie down and try to think of some new designs for junk jewellery that Saul Laurenson can flood the market with.'

'You do that,' said her father. His smile was an obvious effort and she wished she could have cheered him up, but his forlorn hope that she might become the rich Mrs Laurenson was the most shaming thing she had ever encountered.

She shrivelled at the thought that the men might have discussed her between them. She didn't suppose for a moment that her father would have issued an invitation, 'Come and see Charlotte, and see if you fancy marrying her,' but he had shown Saul her photograph, and he would have sung her praises, and he'd insisted on her dining with them and going house-hunting with Saul yesterday.

All that must have looked as if she was on offer, and she cringed with embarrassment, curled up on the bed. Then suddenly she jack-knifed up, remembering herself, half naked, coming in from sunbathing. How appalling if he imagined she had done that as a turn-on! He couldn't, *no* . . . But she felt as cheapened as though she had been caught scheming away like—like Jo-Ann.

If Jo-Ann heard that Saul was a millionaire and wife-hunting she would be laying siege to the Blue Boar. Maybe Charlotte would tell her, and tell Saul she had told her, then he'd know for sure that Charlotte didn't consider herself a candidate.

If he *was* shopping for a wife what a cold-blooded arrangement that would be. Love wouldn't enter into it. Sex, of course, he probably wanted sons. Passion maybe, but no closeness that wasn't physical, and she had to see

Jeremy tonight, she just had to. The crushed rose she had worn on her velvet robe was lying on the dressing table, and she took it into the bathroom and filled a tumbler with water and put the rose in very gently.

Her car was downstairs in the garage, collected from the Blue Boar, but perhaps she shouldn't drive just yet. She might phone Jeremy and ask him to come here, or she might call a taxi to take her to the theatre.

She wanted to get away for a few hours. Everything here seemed to have gone crazy. It was a madhouse in which she didn't know which way to turn, but if she could be quiet for a while with Jeremy she might get back her sanity.

She phoned for a taxi, to be at the end of the road in fifteen minutes. Then she rang the theatre and left a message telling Jeremy she would see him at his flat. The state she looked, with this great bruise on her forehead, and the way she felt, she couldn't face the rest of the cast and staff at the Little Theatre.

She combed her hair to hide as much damage as possible, put on some lipgloss, picked up her handbag and tried to slip out of the house. If her father or Aunt Lucy caught her she would tell them where she was going, but nobody was going to stop her. Just one more hassle and she would run screaming into the night.

The drawing room door was open and Saul was sitting there. Probably her father was too, and she didn't want to talk to either of them. She wanted to walk quietly out of the house and quickly along the lane. That was why she hadn't let the taxi come here, because she wanted to get away with nobody knowing.

But she stood still, clutching her handbag to her as though it was keeping her afloat in deep water, and their gaze locked. Then she took two steps and stood in the doorway glaring at him. 'What's on your mind?' he asked.

Her father wasn't here, and there was so much on her mind that her head was bursting and the air seemed charged like electricity. 'Why did he tell you the business was in trouble?' she demanded. 'He hadn't seen you in fifteen years. Why you?'

Saul seemed to consider his answer. 'Perhaps because I was around when he reached the stage of not being able to keep it to himself any longer, and once he started it seemed possible that we might come to some arrangement.'

The dark eyes bored into her skull, and she could imagine how Saul Laurenson would learn all he wanted to know, drawing out the confidences. Her father had said that, so far as appearances went, he had hardly changed since he ran his stall on the Thursday market. 'He recognised you after all those years,' she said. 'He said you always had a lean and hungry look.'

'Did he?'

'You know the quotation?'

'I've seen the play.' He sounded amused, and of course he knew Shakespeare's *Julius Caesar*. He might have finished his schooling at sixteen, but he had acquired much more than money since then.

'The lean and hungry man's dagger ended in Caesar's back,' she said. 'You wouldn't be stabbing my father in the back?'

He would be unlikely to admit it if he was, but he looked straight at her. 'I've been hungry in my time, it's something that puts an edge on your dealings, but I prefer to get what I want by fair means.'

Charlotte's throat was so dry that her voice rasped. 'And if fair means don't work how do you go about getting what you want?'

He smiled, eyes hooded. 'You know, in the last ten years, I can't recall one single thing I wanted that I didn't get,' and she backed away, shaking her head as though he had said, 'Come here,' and said hurriedly, 'I'm going to see a friend.'

Saul didn't say anything, but she almost ran from the house, and reaching the end of the road as the taxi came into sight hopped in as it slowed down.

'In a hurry, aren't we?' said the taxi driver. He owned the local garage, a stocky jovial man. 'Running away from home?'

'I'm late for a date,' said Charlotte.

'We can't have that. Chipping Queanton, isn't it?'

'Outside the fish and chip shop in the High Street.'

Bob Reading had known Charlotte all her life, and he chuckled now, 'Is that the best he can do for you, fish and chips?' Then he turned serious. 'Hear you've had a bit of an upset. All right, are you?'

He was talking about yesterday's accident, but Charlotte almost burst into hysterical laughter. Her life had been turned upside down and inside out, you couldn't get a much bigger upset than that, and in the back seat she pressed her clenched fist to her lips for a moment before she said, steadily enough, 'I was shaken, that's all.'

She was shaking inside now, for other reasons. She leaned back, face turned towards the passing countryside, thoughts rushing through her head ... My father has always believed I'm special, but Saul Laurenson doesn't. He may be looking for a wife, but he isn't going to choose me, and if by some crazy quirk he did I could say no. I would say that I loved Jeremy. No, no, *no*, I would say ...

She did love Jeremy. Love made you happy and kept you safe. Saul Laurenson was darkness and danger. He was someone she had to fight every inch of the way, not giving a step, because if he got too close God only knew what might happen to her.

They came to the town and passed Dunscombes, its windows alight and glittering behind the protective grilles, and Charlotte looked at the name above, in gold on black, and thought, That may be changed. She would be sad if it were, but it was no longer the business she was fearful for.

Trade was brisk at the fish and chip shop. The door at the side, with two bells, was closed, but they had a key for the flat at the shop and Charlotte went inside, skirting the queue and waiting to catch the eye of someone behind the counter.

She was spotted by a couple in the queue first. Young men, in jeans and T-shirts that read 'I'm Yours', and 'Young Farmers Do It Better', who eyed her up and down and pronounced, 'Tasty.'

Then the man serving saw her, and Charlotte signalled, 'Could I have the key to the flat?'

'Come through.' He lifted the flap of the counter. 'The wife's in.' He knew that Charlotte was Jeremy Wylde's girl, and she went through the door into a living room, where a boy was doing homework on the table and a woman was sewing and watching television.

There was a slight flurry while Mrs Soskins fished in the sideboard drawer for the key. She thought Charlotte and Jeremy made a lovely pair, but this was the first time that Charlotte had arrived to be let into the flat to wait for Jeremy, and Mrs Soskins was intrigued. Then she spotted the bruise under the fringe and another five minutes passed while Charlotte explained how that had come about.

Ten-year-old Stephen was impressed by the bruise. His eyes gleamed. 'Cor, you must have gone a smacker into that windscreen! You could have cut your head off!'

'He watches too much telly,' said his mother complacently. 'Sure you won't have a cup of tea? They're not usually back much before half past ten.'

Of course Peter lived here too, he would probably be with Jeremy, so there would be things Charlotte couldn't say until she had Jeremy to herself, maybe on the way home.

She said, 'Thank you, but I'll go up and wait for them if I may.' The Soskins owned the flat, but the actors paid the rent, and Charlotte Dunscombe was a highly respectable young lady. Mrs Soskins said of course she could and handed over the key, and let Charlotte into the hall from which the stairs led to the first floor flat, switching on the light for her.

Charlotte had never opened this door before. It took her a moment to get the knack of the lock, while Mrs Soskins waited below until the door swung open. Then Mrs Soskins turned off the light and the hall went dark and Charlotte stepped into the shadowy room.

She had been here often enough for the shadows to seem familiar, and she wished it was her key and she could stay. Her home didn't feel safe any longer, while Saul Laurenson was there. She would have liked somewhere like this for a hiding place.

The room was medium sized, furnished comfortably, lit by the lighted street, and Charlotte settled herself in a chair by the window. There were plenty of people about. She watched, with an elbow on the sill and her chin cupped in her hand, and it was like a street scene in a play. Before long Jeremy would come down the road from the direction of the theatre and she would have to explain what had been urgent enough to bring her here tonight.

If the two men returned together she would say she'd got bored, lying resting when there was nothing wrong with her, and the roses were lovely and she'd thought she would just pop over and say thank you. Later she would tell Jeremy about Saul Laurenson, that she didn't trust him or like him and that she had suddenly had to get away from him.

She gasped and leaned forward, her forehead touched the glass of the window and she muttered, 'Ouch!' There was a tall man in the doorway of the shop opposite, and for a moment she thought he was looking up at this window and that he was Saul. Then she saw he was one of a group of young folk, larking about, and you would have to be blind as a bat to imagine a resemblance between him and Saul Laurenson. There was nothing wrong with Charlotte's eyes, but even when she closed them Saul Laurenson's face seemed etched on her lids like a mirror image.

She thought, I'm getting a persecution mania, imagining him coming after me; she pulled the curtains and switched on the light and went into the kitchenette to see what she could find in the fridge. She wasn't hungry, although she hadn't eaten much today, it was just something to do. But she helped herself to a slice of pork pie and a glass of white wine from an opened bottle.

The flat was rather stuffy, the wine was cool and refreshing and more palatable than the pie, which tasted stale. After a mouthful of pie she dropped it into the waste bin and took the wine back into the living room where a tape-recorder, with a script and phone beside it, stood on a low table.

Jeremy and Peter sometimes learned their lines by speaking them into the recorder and listening to the playback. This was a new play. Charlotte read a little, then turned on the recorder and listened to the readings. Peter had a good strong voice, he was a good actor, but she thought that Jeremy sounded infinitely more dramatic. His voice had all sorts of thrilling nuances, and it was pleasant sitting here, sipping her wine and listening.

Peter was speaking when she heard a whirring-clicking sound, followed by Jeremy's voice in the background saying, 'Hello, love, I got your message, are you coming round later?' and realised that this must have been when he phoned her yesterday.

She listened to his comments, remembering her own ... 'I'll kill him!' Jeremy was saying, '... risking your neck. He should have seen the other car.' Then she'd talked about the high hedges and the other driver coming out on to the main road ... 'What were you doing in his car anyway?' And she had explained and teased, 'You wouldn't be jealous?' 'Not so long as you still think he looks like Dracula,' said Jeremy.

Of course tape-recorders were all over the place these days, but this was a little spooky, hearing a few moments she had thought gone for ever being re-enacted. She heard the click as the phone was put down and Peter asked, 'What was all that about?'

'Charlotte was in a car crash.' No mistaking the concern in Jeremy's voice, nor the shock in Peter's, 'My God!'

'She's all right.'

'Thank God for that,' said Peter fervently. 'So what was that about Dracula?'

'The man who was with her,' said Jeremy.

'And what *was* she doing in his car?'

'He's looking for a house, going round property.'

'And she was looking with him?' A bantering note had crept into Peter's voice. 'I'd watch out for him if I were you. There aren't many girls like Charlotte around, lovely *and* loaded, and you always did have expensive tastes.'

Jeremy said, 'Too true,' and Charlotte thought, I'm not loaded any more. Not that it would make any difference to the way Jeremy felt about her, but it would make a world of difference to her life, and she switched off the recorder and wondered what tomorrow would bring. She hoped she was a survivor, but the unknown quantity was Saul Laurenson and how far his influence would shape her future.

She jumped up and poured herself another glass of wine, then paced the room and longed for Jeremy. But when the phone rang she hesitated, then reached very slowly for the receiver. It was Jeremy, to say he would be with her within minutes and was she all right?

'I am now,' she said. When the phone rang she had thought, Saul! although there was no way it could have been. She went on walking, up and down, her nerves a-jangle. There was a big old framed mirror on one wall, that had once hung in a shop and had an advertisement for Monkey Brand Soap etched on it. She glanced at her reflection as she passed, and then over her shoulder, still at the mirror image, as though somebody could have been following close behind.

Of course nobody was, she was quite alone, but she was still very shaken. There had been too many shocks, one on top of the other, and when she heard the footsteps on the stairs she opened the door and called, 'Jeremy, is that you?'

She could see him as she called, but she needed the reassurance of his voice, and when he reached her he exclaimed, 'Hey, darling, you look terrible!' She felt pale and her forehead was throbbing. His stage make-up had been hurriedly and sketchily removed, there were still traces of the lines that had been drawn to make the face of the character he was playing, and any other time she would have smiled at that, teased him for being in such a hurry to come to her. But now she was on the edge of tears, she could easily have fallen sobbing into his arms, and as he led her back into the room and seated her again on the sofa she said shakily, 'The roses were lovely, just lovely, and I had to see you.'

'That bruise!' He lifted her hair very gently from her forehead and she was trembling. 'My poor darling,' he said, 'you could have been killed! I've thought of nothing else since you phoned. I need a brandy.' He poured two large measures and as Charlotte sipped hers it steadied her, that and having Jeremy beside her, his arm around her, kissing her tenderly.

'Where's Peter?' she asked after a few minutes.

'Gone to some party.' He smiled his flashing actor's smile. 'Won't be back till late.'

That was tactful of Peter. Late could mean breakfast-time, and she breathed in the smell of cold cream and greasepaint and the tonic Jeremy used on his hair, then she thought how much she loved him and murmured, 'I wish I could stay here.'

'Why not?' He probably thought she had come to stay. She had never come so late before, and it was tempting but she had to say, 'No, I've got to go back.' Her voice came out husky and he looked closely at her and said, 'You sound almost frightened.'

'Do I?' She smiled as though that was nonsense, but a moment afterwards she admitted, 'Perhaps I am. Dracula's at home.' She was making a joke of it, and Jeremy said, 'Tell me about Dracula.'

She closed her eyes, then took a deep breath and began, 'He's a local boy made good. Very good. From a stall on the market to being at least a millionaire. He's thirty-four and he's a bachelor and he told my father he's tired of being a bachelor, and my father thinks——'

'Not you?' Jeremy interrupted harshly. 'Your father isn't matchmaking with you?'

'My father thinks it would be nice.'

'And what do you think?' Jeremy's face was near hers, she knew that, she could feel it, but she couldn't open her eyes because her lids had become very heavy. 'I think it's impossible,' she said.

'Well, I'm certainly glad to hear that.' But unless she opened her eyes, which she managed to do at last, and stared at Jeremy, she kept seeing Saul.

'But,' she said, 'he has the power.'

'What power?'

'Like Dracula. The eyes!' She drawled that, and made her voice sound like the old retainer's warning in a horror film. 'Would you be closing the window and hanging up some garlic, because I have this notion that he could come flying in?'

'Darling,' said Jeremy, 'you're tipsy.'

'Only a very little.' She was keeping up her spirits because she was afraid of the things that were happening to her. She must do something positive, assert herself, and she looked into Jeremy's long-lashed eyes and asked, 'Do you want to marry me?'

He said, almost at once, 'You know I do,' and she began to smile.

'Now that makes me feel very good, very warm and happy instead of cold and shivery.' She slid her arms round his neck and his arm went round her waist. 'Can I stay?' she asked.

'You certainly can!' His lips muzzled her neck, tickling, and she began to giggle, then sat back a little.

'I'd better phone Aunt Lucy and tell her I'm all right. She could be sending out search parties.' She stretched for the phone and dialled carefully, one hand holding on to Jeremy.

Her father answered. Aunt Lucy would probably be in bed, it was her bedtime, but Charlotte would have preferred to speak to her. Her father's voice threw her a little. In her hazy state she had been all set to reassure Aunt Lucy that she was staying with friends, and was perfectly all right, and would be home in the morning. But her father almost shouted, 'Charlotte, where the devil are you?'

He had no right to shout at her. He had never shouted or lost his temper before Saul Laurenson came. She asked, 'Is Saul still there?'

'Yes.'

That settled it. She was not going back tonight. Saul Laurenson must be listening to her father shouting at her as though she was a naughty child. She said, loud and clear, and hoped Saul was near enough to hear that too, 'I am with a friend. With Jeremy Wylde. And I could be staying for quite a while, because we're getting married. And you can tell Mr Laurenson that, in case he has the impression that I'm part of a business deal.'

She put down the phone and Jeremy said, 'Your father?'

'Mmm.'

'How do you think he's going to take that?'

Suddenly she was almost sober. She said, 'Better in the morning than he will tonight. I don't think I should have told him tonight, not like that.'

The phone rang and the sound stabbed through her head. 'I can't,' she said, and Jeremy answered, with a laconic, 'Yeah,' and, 'O.K. Peter,' he explained, hanging up. 'The flat's all ours. He's dossing down where the party is.'

Charlotte gulped, 'Are you expecting any more calls?'

'No.'

'Then would you mind leaving the receiver off?'

He lifted it from its cradle and laid it on the script of the new play. His address and number were in the book at home and she didn't want to talk to her father again tonight. Nor to Aunt Lucy. Nor to anyone. The little strength she had left was draining out of her as the euphoria of the alcohol went cold. She said, 'I'll have to lie

down, and I'll have to go to sleep.' Her smile was wobbly.
'I feel as though I've been in a head-on collision!'

Jeremy couldn't have been nicer. He gave her his own
bed. He said he'd take Peter's. Charlotte slipped off her
shoes and dress and slid between the sheets, and by now
her headache was raging and her stomach was churning,
and she was feeling too rotten to care what happened
tomorrow . . .

Another ringing woke her, but it wasn't the telephone
and she heard Jeremy, in the darkness, asking who the
hell this was at this time. He turned on a light and went
out of the bedroom into the living room, shrugging his
naked shoulders into a dressing gown.

Charlotte sat up, hardly breathing, straining to hear as
Jeremy threw open the window and called down, 'What
do you want? Who is it?' She heard the answer. 'I've
come for Charlotte,' and she croaked, 'It's Saul!'

Jeremy gasped, 'Your father wouldn't send him to fetch
you, would he?'

'No,' she said. But he had.

'Well, he has,' said Jeremy. 'I'll have to let him in,
he'll be waking half the street, he's probably woken the
Soskins already.'

For a moment Charlotte was paralysed, then furious,
because this was intolerable. She got out of bed, standing
still fighting nausea, then looking around for her dress.
Saul came into the living room ahead of Jeremy, he must
have walked past him in the hall or on the stairs. He
seemed to tower over Jeremy, although in fact they were
about the same height. Jeremy was blustering, 'What the
hell is this?' but Saul took no notice of him. He looked at
Charlotte, standing just inside the doorway of the bedroom, and said, 'Get dressed.'

'You can't come barging in here!' Jeremy's voice was
shrill.

Charlotte pulled her dress over her head and came into the living room where her shoes lay beside the sofa, and all the time she was growing colder, icily sober, filled with the conviction that something was terribly wrong. Jeremy was still talking, she wasn't listening to Jeremy. She slipped into her shoes and faced Saul and asked, 'What's happened?'

'Your father's had a heart attack.'

'I don't believe you.' That was a stupid thing to say. Nobody would tell you a thing like that unless it was true. She turned blindly to pick up her handbag and Jeremy said, 'I'll take you,' but she shook her head. 'No, you mustn't come.'

He kissed her cold cheek and she felt Saul grip her arm, pulling her away. 'Ring me,' said Jeremy, and she nodded and thought, Why? you can't help.

She stumbled on the stairs. She might have fallen, but Saul held her still, opening the car door and letting her slump into the passenger seat. It was like hitting the windscreen had been, a numbing, paralysing blow. As he got into his seat, behind the wheel, she whispered, 'Is it true?' and he looked at her, without any expression at all, but his voice was brutal.

'There's no other reason why I should be getting you out of your lover's bed in the middle of the night.'

She wasn't sleeping with Jeremy, but it didn't matter. She swallowed, tried to speak and couldn't, and tried again, 'How—bad?'

'Bad enough.'

This seemed like a ghost town, with not a soul in sight, everything cold and lonely. She couldn't look at Saul, and each word came separately, each needing an effort. 'Is—he—dead?'

'If he were,' said Saul, 'there'd be no point in my fetching you.'

That was something. He was alive, and while there was life . . . She whispered, 'Please get me to him.' Then she sat huddled, shivering, and after a few moments she managed to ask, 'When did it happen?'

'Just after your phone call. When you told him you weren't coming back home, that you were marrying your actor.'

She had known that would shock her father, but she had never realised that a shock might do him physical harm and she protested wildly, 'But he's never ill. He plays golf, squash.'

'I doubt if he's played much squash lately,' said Saul. 'Didn't you know that either, that his heart was weak?'

She knew that Dr Buckston was always urging him to take things easier, but she thought he gave that advice to all his middle-aged patients in these harassing times. She asked, 'How long have you known?'

'Since we met in Antwerp.'

'He told you.' She could feel tears burning behind her eyes, but she would do no weeping in front of this man and her voice was rough with unshed tears. 'He told you about the business, he told you he had heart trouble. Maybe that was why he didn't need to tell me anything, because he'd found someone else to confide in.' What had happened tonight was her fault, because she hadn't known. 'Somebody should have told me,' she wanted to scream, but it sounded like a whimper.

Saul said, 'You should have known.'

'*How?*' In the last few days she had realised that her father was looking older, but until then she was sure there had been no signs.

'By thinking of somebody else for a change besides yourself,' he said savagely. 'The man's been in hell. God, you make me sick!'

Charlotte didn't care what he said to her. A man who

would talk this way to a girl whose father might be dying
had no pity, and she looked at the hard lines of his profile
and hated him. She wouldn't have run to Jeremy tonight
if this intruder hadn't been in her home. She wouldn't
have said she was marrying Jeremy if her father hadn't
thought Saul might want to marry her. She thought, if
my father dies I'll never have to look at you again; then
she turned away and said no more, and prayed and
prayed.

She should have realised her father would be in hospital, where the best care and treatment could be
provided, but she had expected to be taken home. It
wasn't the hospital Saul had brought her to after the accident. She had never been inside a hospital in her life till
then, and now it was twice within hours. Her father was
in there, and she had helped to put him there, and if she
was given the chance she would take care of him.

She opened her door, as they drew up in the car park,
running ahead of Saul into the hospital. Aunt Lucy sat in
the foyer, Dr Buckston beside her. Her eyelids were swol-
len with tears and Charlotte took hold of her hands,
gripping them tightly, before she turned to the doctor. He
said the blessed words, 'He should pull through this time,'
and that was a prayer answered. 'But he's a sick man.'

The tears on Aunt Lucy's face were relief and grief.
She was clinging to Charlotte, and Charlotte felt her
childhood slipping away and knew that she had to be the
comforter. 'We can nurse him, can't we?' she said. 'We
still have him. We'll make him follow doctor's orders.'
She forced herself to sound calm and steady, her eyes
meeting the doctor's. 'Why didn't you tell me he had a
weak heart?'

'I didn't know,' Aunt Lucy wept.

'Nobody knew,' said the doctor. 'He didn't want you
worrying, Charlotte. I think he's always been over-pro-

tective about you because you look like your mother and she was delicate. He always had to take care of her, and even then he lost her.'

Charlotte said, 'I'm not delicate. Can I see him?'

'He's been asking for you. Just look in on him and reassure him and then we'd better take this lady home.' He patted Aunt Lucy's hand, and she sat huddled in her seat, a handkerchief to her eyes, while he led the way down a corridor. Saul was walking with them and Charlotte said sharply, 'Why are you coming?'

'It's all right,' said the doctor. 'Your father wants to see Mr Laurenson as well.'

Her father's bed was near the door; there were other beds. Little round discs were attached to his chest and wired to a machine beside a small screen, and Charlotte wanted to fling her arms around him, to give him her youth and her strength. She hated herself for having hurt him in any way, and when he saw her and smiled faintly she smiled back although the unshed tears were blinding her.

'It'll be all right,' he whispered.

'I know,' she said. 'You'll be home soon. Oh, you frightened us!'

'Sorry about that.' His gaze moved to Saul, standing just behind her. 'I can't remember much about it, but I'm glad you weren't alone, I'm glad Saul was with you.'

He thought they had been at home together when he was struck down, so he didn't recall the phone call, and that was to the good. She stooped and kissed his cheek and said, 'You must sleep now.'

'And you must all go home. You'll take care of her, won't you?' Again his eyes met Saul's, and he said,

'Of course.'

'Stay with them,' said Colin Dunscombe weakly. 'They'll need a man about the house.'

As soon as she got home Charlotte put Aunt Lucy to bed, dosing her with the tranquillisers that Dr Buckston had provided. She protested that she had never taken a sleeping pill in her life, but Charlotte said, 'Tonight we do. Get yours down now.'

Aunt Lucy swallowed her two pills with the half glass of milk that Charlotte was holding out to her, then Charlotte took her upstairs, seeing her into her bedroom and kissing her goodnight.

Saul had brought them home. He was still downstairs in the kitchen, and he was probably going to sleep in the guestroom, because she could hardly suggest he go back to his hotel at this hour.

She picked up the tiny packet of pills from the kitchen table and put them on the dresser shelf, and he asked, 'Aren't you taking yours?'

'No.' Waking or sleeping she needed to keep her wits about her. He had boiled a kettle and was stirring a cup of instant coffee. 'Coffee?' he asked.

'No, thank you.' She hoped she would sleep, but she knew she wouldn't if she drank any coffee. Saul was making himself at home, the man about the house. She said, 'Please don't consider yourself bound by that ridiculous promise to my father about taking care of me. I can look after myself.'

'I'm sure,' he said, and went on stirring the black coffee, asking conversationally, 'By the way, what's wrong with the man you're marrying?'

She said coldly, 'Absolutely nothing.'

'Well, the news hit your father hard.' He didn't need to remind her of that, and her resentment against him rose dangerously, making her reckless, so that when he asked, 'Why did you break it to him like that?' she said,

'To show him that I've made my own choice. He seemed to think I might be in the running with you.'

He echoed, 'In the running?'

'As you've decided it's time you settled down. As you're wife-hunting. My father, you see, has this funny idea that I'm irresistible.' She wanted him to sneer at that so that she could hit back. She wanted a chance to tell him her opinion of him, but he said shortly,

'That isn't his only mistake. The last thing I want is a wife.'

'Oh!' She turned scarlet. Saul must have said *something*. Perhaps it was to do with buying a house round here, a home, and her father, desperate to find her a protector, had decided a wife went with a home.

'I shouldn't mention Jeremy Wylde to him again for a while if I were you,' said Saul, and Charlotte knew that she must not. Part of the nursing and care for her father would be to keep him quiet and content, and his mind would only be easy if he believed that she and Saul Laurenson were growing closer.

She looked at Saul with a mixture of appeal and horror, and he shrugged as though he read her mind, and said, 'If it will keep him happy over the next few weeks I'll pretend we're getting on like a house on fire.'

His smile was sardonic because he knew that nothing was less likely. 'But if you'd prefer a running battle,' he added, 'that's all right by me.'

'No. No, he wants us to be—friends.' He wanted them to be married lovers, and she shivered, and Saul drank several gulps of coffee, then put down the cup and asked,

'May I use the room I had on Monday?'

'Yes.'

He passed her, going to the door, and stood looking down at her, and she tried to stare back at him without flinching, willing him to go, to just get out. Saul smiled again, a slow smile. 'Not to worry,' he said, 'I don't think you're irresistible any more than I think you need looking after. I think that the only soft thing about you is your skin.'

He ran a fingertip down her cheek and Charlotte turned to stone, cold to the bone. But after he had closed the door behind him her cheek began to burn, and she rubbed hard but she couldn't rub away the memory of his touch. Not even when her cheek was pressed against the pillow and she was trying to sleep.

CHAPTER SIX

AUNT LUCY was still sleeping soundly when Charlotte looked into her bedroom just after seven o'clock next morning. The drug was still working, and she needed all the rest she could get, so Charlotte closed the door softly and crept away. She herself had hardly slept at all, and her one thought now was to phone the hospital for the latest bulletin on her father.

If the phone had rung in the night she thought her own heart would have stopped before she could answer it, but there had been no calls, so her father was still holding his own, and she went downstairs to the hall phone. She was carrying Georgy and when she put him down he trotted off towards the kitchen and the barking retrievers. By this time, on an ordinary day, Aunt Lucy would have been bustling around in the kitchen. The house was strangely still this morning.

As Charlotte picked up the phone Saul said, 'I have rung. He had a fairly good night.' That could mean anything, and she would ring herself in a few minutes and see if she could get more information. Saul was shaved and dressed, she was still in her dressing gown herself, and she said,

'You get up early.'

'I don't need much sleep.' He had come out of her father's office, but she didn't care about that, all she wanted to know was,

'Is he going to live?'

'I'm no doctor.'

'No, of course you're not, how would you know? I just

want somebody to tell me he is.' She had to keep her self-control, there were things to be done, so she asked, 'Would you mind if we talked business?'

That must sound cold-blooded, but unless she started thinking about something else she could go to pieces. 'Not at all,' he said, and she went ahead of him into the kitchen, filled the kettle and lit the gas, hardly conscious of what her hands were doing, any more than she was of the dogs leaping around her.

'I would like you to explain,' she said in a high light voice, 'how the firm managed to get to the edge of bankruptcy when everything looks all right?'

Saul had seated himself at the table. It was quite a domestic scene, he ready to leave for the office, she still in her dressing gown, as though they had shared the same bed and would now be sitting down together to breakfast. It was all unreal. Charlotte thought wildly, perhaps it is a nightmare and if I put my hand in that flame my skin won't burn.

Behind her he said, 'The business has been losing money for years and your father had to cut into capital. Then, when the capital had gone, and he learned that he had a heart condition, he began speculating, shares and horses. He wanted to provide for you, to leave you comfortably off.' He didn't think she was worth such a sacrifice, and neither did she, and if she had known what was happening she would have stopped it.

She didn't look at Saul. She stood with her back to the table, waiting for the kettle to boil, arms folded and fingers gripping. 'He wasn't lucky?' she said.

'You could say that. Not in his investments nor his daughter.'

'So you bought us out? And as we were on the rocks I'm sure you got us cheap. Do we have any money?'

'I doubt it. There were debts to be met.'

'Well, well.' So they were broke, but it hardly seemed to matter. The kettle screamed and she went through the motions of making tea, slowly, as though this was a demonstration, and behind her Saul said,

'Do you understand what I'm telling you?'

She fetched milk from the fridge, and poured it into two of the three cups that Aunt Lucy had put here last night when she laid the table for breakfast. That would be before Charlotte's father collapsed. 'Oh God,' prayed Charlotte, 'let my father come home.'

She said, 'Sure I understand, but hearing we're poor seems much less important than whether my father will come home again. I suppose——' the thought struck her as she was pouring the tea and suddenly her hand was unsteady, 'I suppose we do have a home? I mean, was this part of his capital?'

'The house and grounds are mortgaged to the hilt,' said Saul.

Charlotte put down the teapot quickly. A great weight seemed to have descended on her. She knew now how her father had felt, standing at her bedroom window last night, shoulders and head bowed. She asked, 'To you?'

'No.'

'That means we'll have to get out, because we can't meet big mortgage repayments. We probably couldn't manage the upkeep anyway—rates, electricity.' Her hair felt heavy as a helmet and she pushed it back from her forehead and winced. She had thought she was lucky not going through the windscreen, and she was, but more bad luck was waiting for her than she would have believed possible. If they had no home, no money, where was she going to take her father?

She said, 'The furniture?' She looked through the door leading into the hall and the other rooms. 'Does that still belong to us? Nothing's gone. You can't take out a mortgage on furniture, can you?'

'No,' he said, 'but——'

'But someone could buy it and not have taken it away yet?'

'Yes.'

'You?' He nodded. 'How was that done?'

'A valuer, an agreed price.'

Her father had been selling everything for her sake. Gambling to make her future secure and losing everything. He had been such a fool, and all because he loved her. She said shakily, 'I suppose the final gamble was me, that I'd find myself a rich husband. No wonder he couldn't have me falling in love with a hard-up actor!' She threw back her head and almost laughed, and wondered if she was going out of her mind. 'If he'd told me sooner that I should be fortune-hunting I might have managed it, you know, because I'm a good-looker. Not much else. The packaging's good, but you were right about the I.Q. and you were right that I should have known that he was ailing and so was the business. Only I didn't. And now we've got nothing, or next to nothing. You haven't bought the lot, have you? There must be a few pieces left. Would you care to walk round with me and tell me what belongs to you so that——'

The phone began to ring, silencing her as though a hand had been clapped over her mouth. When she found her voice again there was no hysteria in it. It was almost a whisper, 'Please, would you answer that?'

She followed Saul into the hall. He gave the number and then held out the phone to her and said, 'Jeremy Wylde.'

'Oh, darling!' She almost fell on it. 'Oh, I thought you were the hospital. He's ill, he's very ill, but they said he had a fairly good night.'

Jeremy said how sorry he was, and was there anything

he could do, and she wanted to tell him about Dunscombes and the house and that she didn't know which way to turn, but Saul Laurenson was listening, so she said, 'I'll ring you later.'

'I love you,' said Jeremy.

'Oh, I love you,' she told him, 'and I'll ring you back.' She put down the phone and looked at Saul and said, 'I'm sorry I started ranting just now. I do realise it's going to be tough, but I'll cope somehow so long as he's going to be all right.' She began to plan. 'I must find out exactly what the overheads are and then I'll get organised. We could do bed-and-breakfast, perhaps evening meals too, Aunt Lucy and I. She's a superb cook and I'm a good one. I'll spread out what's left of the furniture and go round the auctions.'

She had to keep telling herself that her father would live and she would work and it was going to be all right. 'What did you buy?' she asked. 'What is left?'

Saul said, 'I've a proposition you might consider,' and she stiffened. 'I like this house,' he said. 'I'd consider paying off the mortgage, and taking on the running expenses. I should want to choose my rooms, but I wouldn't be using them for more than a few weeks in the year. You and your family could go on living here and the house could stay the way it is.'

Only yesterday she had run from the house because he was in it, and now he was suggesting that he should buy it and they should become his lodgers or his guests, and she was so desperate that she was grateful. Her father could come back here, and she could deal with the problems before her calmly, with the biggest problem of all solved. She said huskily, 'That sounds wonderful. It's very kind of you. If my father can get well anywhere it would be here.'

'It isn't kindness,' he said, and she thought, No, it

wouldn't be, so what would you want in payment?

He went back to the kitchen, a tall athletic man walking through what was soon to be his own property. So long as he doesn't consider I am, thought Charlotte. To keep her family under this roof she would pay almost any price, but all she had to pay with was herself. A few days ago she could never have envisaged a situation like this, but now as she followed him she thought, I've no right to pride. When he tells me his price, if that's what he wants, I'll grit my teeth and pay.

She sat down at the kitchen table, pulled a cup of tea towards her and said, 'Well, I'm glad you like the house.'

'I always did,' he said. 'I came up here once in the old days. Your father bought some saddles from me and I brought them up. I always remembered the house.' He grinned, 'I was living in a van at the time,' and Charlotte wondered if he had resented and envied her father.

When the two men met again years later, and Saul Laurenson learned that Colin Dunscombe was facing ruin, the change in their fortunes might have gratified him. He could be getting a kick out of owning the business, and now the house. There wasn't much left around here that he didn't own, and she said, 'If you let us go on living here, how much—I mean, what would you——?' She floundered, and he looked straight into her eyes and it was as though he took possession of her without touching. 'We'll discuss it later,' he said, and Charlotte stumbled to her feet, reaching for the teapot, pouring another cup and muttering about taking it up to Aunt Lucy.

Aunt Lucy woke sluggishly. She blinked at Charlotte, then remembered, and her face puckered as she struggled to sit up. 'He had a good night,' said Charlotte. 'I'm going to see him this morning.' She had just phoned the hospital again and they had told her his condition was satisfactory. She wouldn't really know until she saw him, but she was putting on a show of confidence for Aunt Lucy's sake.

Aunt Lucy looked older too this morning. Her round face seemed to have caved in, and there were shadows round her eyes as she looked reproachfully at Charlotte. 'You shouldn't have gone off like that. He was worried about you, what with the accident.' Charlotte's pallor, and the bruise still scarring her forehead, brought a gentler note to Aunt Lucy's voice. 'You should have been resting, not gadding about. He was asking for you in the ambulance.'

Charlotte said miserably, 'I went to say thank you for the roses.'

'Yes,' said Aunt Lucy, 'well, that can't be helped now, can it? But what we should have done if Mr Laurenson hadn't been there——' Words failed her. 'And at the hospital,' she said, 'when he started asking for you again, Mr Laurenson said he'd come back here and fetch you.'

She thought Charlotte was home by then, that she would have slipped in and gone up to her room, not realising the house was empty. She didn't know about the phone call. There was a great deal more she didn't know, and this was no time to tell her.

Charlotte said, 'Saul's staying on here,' and Aunt Lucy smiled for the first time and began to drink her tea.

I wonder if I could model, Charlotte thought as she dressed. She had always been told she could. When she had modelled Dunscombe jewellery the advertisements had been produced by an agency who had said they could get her other work, but even if that was a genuine offer professional modelling was fiercely competitive. Even if she was lucky she would have to be mobile and available, and it might be months before she could leave her father, just like that.

So she would have to find work locally, and she had no doubt that she could because she was prepared to turn her hand to anything legal. She would have to ask around. She had friends who owned shops, hotels, garden centres, a riding school. Maybe Jeremy could suggest something; she had to tell him what was happening here.

She dialled his number on the hall phone and he answered at once. 'I was just going to ring you,' he said. 'Would you like me to come over? I don't like to think of you being on your own.'

She would have liked that, but she said, 'I'm going to the hospital at ten and then I don't know what I'll be doing. It seems my father's sold out.'

Jeremy was puzzled. 'You mean the shop, the works?'

'Yes.'

'But you didn't know anything about that, did you?'

'Nobody did.' She couldn't help sounding bitter. 'Except Saul Laurenson, and some lawyers, I suppose.'

Jeremy said, 'Well, obviously it was getting too much for him. This heart attack proves it was time he retired.'

'It wasn't by choice. We've gone broke, bust. Even the house is mortgaged.'

'You're joking!'

Charlotte shook her head as though he could see her, and heard the stairs creaking under Aunt Lucy's weight, and said, 'It's no joke and I need a job.'

'I can't believe it!' Jeremy sounded as if he was gasping for air, and Charlotte heard herself say, quite lightly, 'Well, that's the way of it. I have to go now, love,' and she rang off and waited for Aunt Lucy to reach the bottom of the stairs.

Aunt Lucy flung herself into the household chores, cooking breakfast although Charlotte protested that she couldn't possibly face bacon and eggs. 'Mr Laurenson will,' said Aunt Lucy. 'A man needs a proper meal to start the day. Your father likes his breakfast.' She placed four slices of bacon in the pan and Charlotte went out to the stables, before the aroma of frying could reach her and her queasy stomach, and saddled Kelly.

As she galloped she wondered if Kelly still belonged to her. If Saul had come up here selling saddles presumably he appreciated good horseflesh when he saw it. If he had been in the market for antique furniture her father might have put a price on Kelly too.

Well, that was one sale that wouldn't go through. She was keeping Kelly, if she had to ask Mary from the riding school to give him stabling. She went fast over the fields, her hair blowing across her face, into her eyes. Her eyes were stinging, tears filling them, and she let herself weep until she turned for home. Then there were no more tears and those she had wept dried on her cheeks.

Maudie and Tom had arrived by the time she got back. Neither had heard the ambulance in the night and they were both in the kitchen, groggy with shock. 'Who'd have thought it?' old Tom, biting on his empty pipe, was saying dolorously. 'Who'd have thought it? Nearly twenty years I could give him.'

Maudie was recalling an uncle of hers, who had looked the picture of health and dropped dead, and Aunt Lucy said sharply, 'He isn't dead, he's going to be all right.'

'Of course he is,' said Maudie. 'Mind you, he'll never be the same again.' Then they saw Charlotte and began to tell her about the wonders of modern medicine and that her father would be home in no time.

Saul went with her to the hospital. She would rather have gone alone, but his car was outside the door and hers was in the garage, and he said, 'Shall we go?' just as she was about to say she was off.

They did no talking on the way, but when Charlotte gave her name and the nurse at the desk said that the doctor would like a word with her she turned to Saul in alarm. It had to be bad news, there had been nothing else. She might have asked if she could go in to see her father alone, but she was glad enough to have Saul with her when she went into the little office.

Behind a desk a bespectacled thin-faced man gave them a professional smile and indicated chairs and said, 'Now, Miss Dunscombe, you do understand that your father is a sick man.' Get on with it, thought Charlotte. Tell me what you have to tell me. 'But so far his progress has been steady,' the doctor went on, and she realised that she was still standing and clutching Saul's arm, so she let go and sat down.

'Dr Buckston says that you can provide facilities for home nursing,' said the doctor. 'That would mean a trained nurse in residence at first.'

Saul said, 'Yes.'

'When?' asked Charlotte.

'He'll be in here for at least a week, nearer ten days I should say, and that of course is presuming that progress is maintained.'

This wasn't bad news. Maybe the worst was over and she could start hoping. She listened intently to every word . . . no worries, no upsets, familiar surroundings . . .

'Yes,' she said, 'yes. May we see him?'

It was 'we' now. Saul Laurenson was going to help her get her father home, and he had said 'Yes' to the trained nurse, so she could set her father's mind at rest about the house.

It was a brief stay. To Charlotte he looked almost as ill as he had last night, but when he saw Saul was with her he smiled, and Charlotte said, 'Saul's told me about everything. He wants to take over the house. He wants——' she swallowed, 'he wants us all to live there.'

When she got outside she said, 'Perhaps I should have

put that differently, about us all living together.'

Saul grinned. 'Wait until he gets stronger, then you can remind him that you're marrying your actor and you can tell him that I'm not a marrying man.'

She wondered how long it would be before her father was strong enough to hear these things, then she thought how pleased Aunt Lucy would be to know he was coming home, and she asked, 'Do you have a family? Parents?'

'No,' he said. 'Shall I take you back to the house?'

'Please. Are you coming back?'

'I'm going to Dunscombes, to put the staff in the picture.'

'Nobody's done that.' Nobody had or she would have known. It had all been hush-hush, and it was going to come as a shock to the men and women who worked there.

'Your father and I were going to explain the changes together,' said Saul.

'The takeover, you mean.'

'Yes.'

'Then you'd better take me along, hadn't you? The last of the Dunscombes.'

She was going to hate this, but her father was coming home, the worst hadn't happened, and now she could face anything. Also she wanted to hear what Saul had to say, what he proposed doing with the business she had thought was safe as the Bank of England but which had been running at a loss for years.

When they turned into Dunscombes' car park a little crowd surrounded them as Charlotte was recognised. The works and office staff had done no work this morning. Since the news reached them that C.D. had gone down with a heart attack in the night, and that Dunscombes could be closing, the employees had been making phone calls—to the house, to the hospital, to the firm's solicitors.

A solicitor was here now, confirming that a change in management was imminent but that he could make no further comment at the moment. He had an appointment to be here and he was waiting in the office.

It had all been anxious speculation, and as Charlotte got out of the car a dozen men, most of them in working overalls, and two girls, descended on her. All of them wanting to know how was her father, and what was happening?

She knew every one of them as well as she knew her own family. The youngest man was Benjy, who had come here from school six years ago and had always had a crush on her. He was a pattern maker and had worked with her on her designs. The oldest was Jan, Polish, thick-set, with big hands that cut and polished the precious stones with meticulous finesse. 'You could trust Jan with an emerald,' Charlotte's father had said. A soft stone, an easy stone to spoil, and for some reason that ran through her head now, while she wondered how she was going to tell them that perhaps they should not have trusted her father.

She said, 'He's very ill. I don't think he'll be working again for a long time. This is Mr Laurenson, he's—well, he's taking over.'

A hush fell. Charlotte hoped that Saul would do the explaining, and he said, 'If you'd come with me,' and led the way from the car park through the back entrance into the salon. They all trooped after him, and as he headed for Colin Dunscombe's office at the front of the shop he said to the senior salesman, 'As soon as you're through with these two ladies,' two women were wandering around, peering into the cases, 'perhaps you and your staff would put up the Closed sign and join us.'

The office was a good-sized room, lush with red flock wallpaper, red Wilton carpet and crystal chandelier. The desk, chairs and cabinets were in Sheraton style, and on the desk were two studio portraits, one of Charlotte, the other of her mother, although strangers always took them for sisters, perhaps twins, both wearing the same gold-filigree-and-aquamarine collar and earrings.

Two men were already in the room: Mr Haden, the firm's lawyer, soberly clad and grave enough for a funeral, and a younger, smarter-looking man. The younger man had been sitting in Colin Dunscombe's chair and he jumped up when Saul walked in. Saul waved him back again, and remained standing as the room filled with a subdued and apprehensive audience.

They were all looking anxiously at each other, at Saul, at Charlotte; and when the sales staff joined them even the murmuring stopped and you could have heard a pin drop.

Charlotte stood by the door, her back to the wall, and she thought, Saul's the only relaxed one here. Even the man who was sitting in her father's chair, because Saul had said that was all right, was turning a pen over and over between his fingers. But Saul sat on the edge of the desk, as casually as though he was chatting with a friend, and when he spoke his voice was quiet and reassuring. But carrying. Nobody was going to miss a word, and Charlotte wondered if that came from addressing board and shareholders' meetings, or whether it went right back to when he had a stall on the market, and bit her lip because he was talking about last night and her father, and she had to stop her lips trembling.

'Colin Dunscombe was going to bring me along to introduce me to you all,' Saul was saying, 'but it will be some time before he's well enough, so I have to introduce myself.'

'Are you taking over the business?' That was Mr Pendleton, the senior salesman, who knew there was no hope of another job at his age if Dunscombes closed down.

When Saul said he was Mr Pendleton, at least, was glad to hear it.

'You're not from round here, are you?' asked the accounts clerk, and when Saul smiled at her she gave a delighted little giggle.

'I was,' he told her, 'until fifteen years ago. I used to have stalls on some of the markets, Stratford, Moreton, selling saddlery and tack.'

Several of them remembered him then and Charlotte thought, It's turning into a reunion. 'Fifteen years ago,' he said, 'I went to Australia. Six months ago I met Mr Dunscombe and he told me he was selling out.'

He hadn't told his staff. There was resentment about that, muttering, but Saul said, 'You must have known orders haven't been coming in, and there've been more how-muchers than buyers in the salon,' and then he had them nodding.

Either he knew the jewellery trade or he had done his homework. His talk was professionally knowledgeable, dealing with problems and prospects. He praised the work they did here. There would always be room for superb craftsmanship. Of course they were proud of their salon, with every good reason, and there was no reason why it shouldn't continue as a showplace.

But he proposed bringing the manufacturing side up to date, so that production was increased, sometimes using semi-precious or man-made stones instead of gems, making prices competitive for a much wider market. He had interests in stores and shops where the goods could go on display in half a dozen countries.

Charlotte watched, feeling like an outsider. He was more than impressive, he had the charisma and confidence of a man who had never failed. He was selling himself to his staff, who had no choice about accepting him because whether they liked it or not he was the boss now, but he would have them eating out of his hand before long. She could understand how reassuring it must be to have someone like Saul Laurenson telling you you were on to a winner, after you had spent most of the morning facing the prospect of unemployment.

She doubted if her father had generated much enthusiasm in his staff lately, and he had never been a Saul Laurenson. Saul was the new breed, the hard men who were the natural inheritors. He was telling them that anyone who wanted to leave the firm would get generous redundancy payments, and she was sure that even Jan—who was past the national retirement age although his hands were still rock-steady—would stay on. Saul didn't actually say, 'Are you with me?' but if he had she would have expected them all to chorus, 'Yes!'

Her voice might have been the only 'No,' and she had less choice than any of them.

The man sitting in her father's chair was Roger Fairley. Saul introduced him as, 'My manager,' which meant he was going to be their manager, and asked if there were any questions, any problems.

You must be joking, thought Charlotte. Have I got problems? Would it be in order for me to ask, 'Is Mr Laurenson expecting me to sleep with him in payment for keeping the old home going?' Her muscles locked and again came that feeling of being trapped and she had to get out of here.

As she slipped through the door from the office into the salon only Saul saw her go. Everyone else was either looking at him, or at Roger Fairley who, in answer to a question, had opened a portfolio and was telling them about Saul's successful business ventures.

If she went across to the theatre she might catch Jeremy, and as she came out of the car park into the road she almost collided with one of his colleagues, an actress about the same age as herself, called Lesley Coltan. She had straight smooth-falling bright red hair, and a complexion so pale that she looked sickly. Jeremy used to make fun of her because more than once she had fluffed her lines, and she almost stammered now, 'I say, I'm so sorry, I mean about your father. Jeremy told me. Isn't it awful? How is he?'

'He'll be all right,' said Charlotte. Each time she told anyone that she was telling herself; and silently, each time, she added, 'Please God.'

'And is it true about the shop?' Lesley's pale grey eyes were fixed on her and Charlotte said, 'The business has been sold.' There was no point dodging the facts and she added, 'Not that my father had much choice. It would have closed down if he hadn't sold it.'

'I am sorry,' said Lesley, giving Charlotte a sad little smile. 'It's funny, isn't it? We thought you were rich, you know, going to help the theatre and everything.'

'I don't know about rich,' said Charlotte wryly, 'but I didn't know what the recession had done to the firm. This has been the eye-opener of the week.'

'And you were in a car accident, weren't you?' Lesley looked for the bruise under the fringe, so Jeremy must have described that as well, and Charlotte was aware of someone looming behind her. As Lesley's gaze switched upwards she turned, almost into Saul's arms.

He'd never followed her out. Well, he must have done, but it could only have been because he was through in there. 'Ready to go?' he asked.

She hesitated, and took the line of least resistance. 'I suppose so. Have you finished?'

'Roger's dealing with the questions.' He led her away from Lesley and she jerked her arm away from him, muttering, 'I do know where the car is.' Then she said, 'Sorry,' because if her father was going to believe they were good friends she mustn't shy at a touch; and if she couldn't bear Saul to touch her how could she contemplate letting him make love to her, if that was his price? She was far from sure that she could, but she would cross that bridge when—if—she came to it.

As they passed Dunscombes, still with the 'Closed' sign up, she asked, 'Will it be making money now?'

'Of course.'

He was so sure of himself, so arrogant, and she asked, 'Does it feel good, coming back and taking over? When you went away did you think you might do this some day?'

He smiled, at his own thoughts. 'Now you mention it, maybe I did.'

'You said you don't have any family—are your parents dead?'

'My mother died when I was sixteen.'

'And your father?'

'I can't remember anyone ever mentioning my father. As my mother was Irish tinker stock it's possible he was too.'

Charlotte said, with a flash of mischief, 'I suppose he didn't come from Transylvania?'

'What?'

'He wasn't a count with very long teeth?'

For a moment he must have thought she was raving, then he burst out laughing and leered at her. 'What great big eyes you have, sweetheart, and what a beautiful white neck!'

She giggled, then had to bite her lip or the giggles might have got out of hand. Hysteria had been just beneath the surface all morning. After that she made an effort to talk rationally. She congratulated Saul on his handling of the meeting just now. 'Although I suppose you were bound to be a success,' she couldn't help adding. 'You'd come to save their jobs, so of course they were glad to see you, especially as you're nearly local and they'll trust a local lad.'

That was ridiculous. He was a man of the world, but he had come back to buy a home here, so he must feel his roots were in this place. She asked, 'Where do you live? Do you have other homes?'

'Apartments,' he told her, 'in various hotels, a stud farm in Australia.' All staffed, of course, as this house would be, with Aunt Lucy and herself running it, cooking, cleaning. Surely that should be return enough for the privilege of living there. He had told her she would have to get into the habit of taking orders, and she observed drily, 'You've come a long way from living in a van.'

'That was a long time ago. Long enough for anyone's life-style to change.'

'Mine changed overnight,' she said. 'And all I want from the future is to be married to Jeremy and have children—two, maybe three.' That wasn't *all* she wanted, but it was a secure domestic picture and it seemed a defense against Saul, who drawled,

'See you don't ruin them like your father did you.'

That was unfair, blaming her again. 'Because you didn't have a happy childhood yourself,' she said hotly, 'don't begrudge me mine. It's not my fault that your mother didn't know who your father was.'

They were drawing up outside the Blue Boar. 'You're right,' he said. 'And if the children take after you they'll be beautiful.' His reversal disarmed her and she said,

'I'm sorry. I know you think I've been spoiled rotten, but I'm not really useless.'

'I'm sure you're not,' he said, and she watched him go inside the hotel. He would be settling up in there, moving into her home, because he had promised her father he would and because he was buying the house. A man came out with him, carrying two suitcases, practically bowing him back into the car. As they drove away Charlotte said cynically, 'You haven't bought the hotel?' He grinned, and she said, 'Just a good tipper?'

'Nobody carries the bags for nothing,' he said, and she heard herself ask, 'Any message from Jo-Ann?' and blinked in surprise, because she hadn't realised she was thinking about Jo-Ann.

'Yes,' he said, and turned on the radio; although if that was to close the subject he need not have bothered, because she wasn't going to ask any more questions.

Tom was working in the garden, trimming the edges of the front lawn, and waiting for them. He came to meet the car as they turned, and Charlotte wound down her window and said, 'He'll be out in about ten days. Then we can have him home.'

Tom nodded, pleased, and as they drove round to the back of the house, the courtyard and the garages, Saul asked, 'You've got another gardener besides him?'

'Me,' she said. He glanced down at her hands, with the aquamarine ring and the polished nails, and she said, 'In gloves. And that's something else I could do for a living. I've got the tools, I think—they didn't go with the furniture, did they? I could keep wild gardens down. That I've had practice in.'

The sound of a vacuum cleaner met them. Maudie was doing the housework. They were all trying to carry on as usual, although Aunt Lucy, in the kitchen, was looking hot and flustered. She said first, 'How is he?' and, when they told her, 'You've been such a time I was beginning to wonder.' And then, 'The dratted phone's never stopped ringing. You'd no sooner gone than it started. Asking me if the business was closing down. I told them pretty sharpish I didn't know, but if it was it wouldn't be before time, seeing the state it's brought Mr Colin to.'

'Saul's taking over,' said Charlotte. 'We went there, after we left the hospital. He's put a new manager in. There are going to be changes.'

'Oh, are there? Changes?' Aunt Lucy sounded as though she suspected Saul Laurenson of harassing Colin Dunscombe into that hospital bed. 'Bit sudden, all this, isn't it?' she said.

'Not really,' said Charlotte, but Aunt Lucy went on glaring at Saul. Her world, like Charlotte's, had collapsed since that man came into this house, and she was remembering now that Charlotte had said at the start that she didn't trust him.

'Young man,' Aunt Lucy began belligerently, 'I don't know what your game is, but——' Charlotte said quickly,

'I'll tell you all about it. Just sit down. We'll both sit down and I'll explain.'

The phone rang again and Saul went out of the kitchen, closing the door behind him, and Charlotte reached across the kitchen table for Aunt Lucy's hands and held them tightly, and said, 'Don't blame Saul.'

'If I knew what was going on——' said Aunt Lucy, and there was no easy way to tell her. Charlotte spoke of falling profits, of investments that hadn't yielded dividends. She didn't mention the horses that had limped home, but she emphasised her father's struggle to provide for her and Aunt Lucy and how the strain had finally broken him. Dunscombes was lucky that Saul Laurenson had been prepared to take over, but there wasn't any money left.

She said, 'It's going to be all right,' and felt this was becoming a repeating refrain. 'I'll get work, we shall manage.'

'We could do something with this place.' Aunt Lucy was less shattered at losing her security than Charlotte had feared, but of course she hadn't heard it all. Charlotte told her, 'He mortgaged the house, he sold most of the furniture,' and went on very fast, '*But* Saul was looking for a house round here and he's going to buy this one; and he's the one who bought the furniture, and he says it can stay the way it is. He'll be responsible for the upkeep, and we can bring my father back here, and we can all stay on. He'll want to choose his rooms, but he'll only be living here for a few weeks in the year.'

That took a while to sink in. Aunt Lucy thought about that, then she said, 'And we look after the place for him?'

'Yes.'

'It's a big place to be keeping on for a few weeks in the year.'

'It's hardly a stately home,' Charlotte protested. 'It's just a nice little Georgian, and he's got the money.'

'Enough to buy anything he fancies, I daresay?' queried Aunt Lucy, suddenly tight-lipped.

'Probably.'

She eased her bulk out of the chair, standing and glaring at Charlotte across the table, announcing, 'I wasn't born yesterday. I know why Mr Laurenson wants me around here—for the cooking and the cleaning. It's what he's got in mind for you that bothers me. Your father won't be much protection to you for a while, but Mr Laurenson needn't think he's moving in here and——'

While she was groping for the words Charlotte suggested,

'Exercising the droit du seigneur?'

'What?' snapped Aunt Lucy.

'She was poor but she was honest,' said Charlotte, and Aunt Lucy snapped,

'You can laugh, but you go right along to him now and you say you'll expect to be treated with respect. Like a lady. And if there's any question of anything else we're getting out of here. I've got a bit put by me, we'll manage.'

Aunt Lucy's savings wouldn't go far in today's world, but Charlotte hadn't the heart to tell her so. If her father hadn't been ill she might have agreed to leave the house and look for a cottage, but his only hope was an untroubled convalescence. He couldn't face upheavals. She said, 'Very well, I'll go and talk to Saul.' She grinned. 'And I'll tell him that Jeremy will kill him if he lays a finger on me!' She had to put Aunt Lucy's mind at rest on this. This was Charlotte's personal problem and she would deal with it herself.

'Don't talk so soft,' said Aunt Lucy, in no way reassured. 'Half a dozen Jeremy Wyldes wouldn't stop Saul Laurenson from crossing the street, let alone from anything he'd set his mind on.'

Charlotte wanted to protest about that. Aunt Lucy hardly knew Jeremy. Nor, for that matter, did she know Saul, but she might be right about one of Saul's motives in buying this house. Charlotte didn't flatter herself that she was his main reason. He liked the house and he could afford it. It might amuse him to be master here, where he had delivered goods from his market stall.

But although there was antagonism between him and Charlotte there was also a physical attraction. She could be part of the bargain, and if she was it must be kept from Aunt Lucy, who would consider it a shocking and terrible price. Aunt Lucy didn't understand how things had changed since she was a girl nearly half a century ago.

All the same, Charlotte went out of the kitchen to look for Saul with a dry mouth and panic fluttering inside her.

He was still on the telephone in the hall, finishing a call. He put down the phone as Charlotte approached and said, 'You'll be wanting this.' A sheet of paper by the phone was covered with jottings, names, numbers, the odd message, in Aunt Lucy's and Maudie's writing. Charlotte noticed that Jeremy had called, and as soon as she had talked with Saul she would sit down and call back the callers.

She said, 'Could you spare me a minute? There's something I want to discuss with you.'

'Of course.'

Then the noise of Maudie's vacuum-cleaner at the top of the stairs stopped, which meant Maudie was probably listening, and Charlotte went across the hall into the drawing room with Georgy at her heels. As Saul followed her into the room she said, 'Aunt Lucy's upset. It's all been such a shock to her. That's why she sounded as though she was about to lay about with her rolling pin just now.'

He grinned, 'Forget it, it was quite a novelty being addressed as "young man".' He was still a young man, but she knew what he meant. She said, 'I've explained to her about the business and that it isn't your fault my father's where he is.'

It was strange in this room, knowing that the house belonged to somebody else and not knowing how much of the furniture did. She couldn't be still. She went to the window, then across to the fireplace, she walked as she talked, while Georgy threaded between her feet, catching her restlessness.

'I've got some jewellery of my own,' said Charlotte. 'I shall sell that and that should pay for the nurse for a while. I can find other things to sell, I'm sure I can, to pay her as long as we need her and to tide us over. And I'm sure I can find work. I do have friends. Somebody will find me something.'

'Modelling, perhaps,' said Saul. He was standing too. He had gone to the window and stayed there, his broad shoulders silhouetted, the slanting light casting shadows on his face.

'I'm not going to take the world of modelling by storm overnight,' she said. 'I've only been an amateur. If I had time and the money didn't matter I might try my luck, but I need to start earning a living right away.'

'Very practical.' She wasn't sure whether he was amused or approving.

'Which brings us,' she went on, 'to the house.'

It brought her to the stage where she couldn't look at him. She had arrived at a glass-fronted corner cupboard, and she began rearranging the contents, moving the little porcelain objects around, with her back to him. 'If you're paying off the mortgage, and paying the upkeep, and letting us live here, we'd sort of become your staff, wouldn't we?'

'Sort of,' he agreed.

'Well, Aunt Lucy is a very experienced housekeeper and cook, so you'd get a bargain there. But you'd hardly need two cooks, so how do you suggest I pay for my lodgings?'

'Be my guest,' he said. But there could be strings to that. She could be so beholden to him that she would be hard pressed to refuse him anything, and she took a deep breath and said bluntly,

'If we're living here, and you're paying, it won't be long before they'll be saying I'm your mistress.'

Her face was flaming, because that was how folk would interpret the situation, and when Saul asked, 'Would that worry you?' she couldn't answer at once. Being his mistress would do more than worry her, it would frighten her to death. She was less sophisticated than she looked. 'What folk say,' he added.

'Oh, that! No.'

'Then what's the problem?'

Charlotte closed the cabinet door and turned to face

him. 'I do do quite a lot of housework, and the gardening, I'd like to carry on with that.'

'Splendid,' he said, and she had misjudged him and so had Aunt Lucy, he didn't hope he was buying Charlotte with the property. That was a tremendous relief, of course. She laughed at herself and said gaily,

'Anyhow, with Aunt Lucy as a chaperone it has to be a respectable set-up.'

'She's a big lady.' His eyes gleamed wickedly. 'It would be a brave man who tried to seduce you with her and her rolling pin around.' He was laughing with her, and it was all she could do not to fling herself into his arms because she wasn't relieved at all that he didn't want her. Because, suddenly and shatteringly, she was realising how much she wanted him.

CHAPTER SEVEN

IT was comfort Charlotte needed, of course. Reassurance. With everything disintegrating around her Saul seemed rock-like. She wanted him to tell her it was going to be all right, and indeed he could hardly be doing more than taking over the business and the house. In his own interests, of course, but the fringe benefits would reach Charlotte and her family.

You only had to look at him to feel that if he was on your side most of your problems would be solved, and she was looking at him. At the springing thickness of the dark hair, the black-lashed eyes under the heavy brows. She knew from the way he moved that he had the body of an athlete, and she looked at the mouth, that could be humorous and cruel; her own lips parted as though under a hard and demanding kiss, and it was more than comfort that she craved.

A raging hunger had seized her to be in Saul's arms. Fighting or loving, but held against him. She wanted the touch of his flesh and hair, and the taste of him on her lips, and her voice rose shrilly. 'I have to phone Jeremy.' She made a dart for the door followed, in a rush, by Georgy.

She rang the flat and Jeremy answered and she began to chatter. She told him that her father would be home within a fortnight, that there was a new manager in Dunscombes, that she had bumped into Lesley Coltan in town.

'Lesley told me,' said Jeremy. 'And she said that somebody, who had to be Dracula, took you away. He does a lot of that, doesn't he?'

'We came back here,' Charlotte explained. 'There's a lot to be done—all sorts of arrangements.'

Jeremy was all sympathy again. 'There must be. Did you say you were losing the house too?'

'Yes and no. It won't belong to us any more, but we can stay on here.' She could see difficulties ahead there, but for the time being they would have to stay on.

'How rotten for you!' Jeremy sighed for her and she couldn't agree more, although it wasn't the end of the world. 'If there's anything I can do—anything,' he said, and she glanced up at Saul, who was tapping his watch and looking impatient.

She said, 'I have to go.'

'I love you,' said Jeremy. They usually finished phone calls that way, and meetings usually.

'And I love you,' she echoed, and of course she did, although Jeremy had never stirred anything in her like those churning emotions just now. That was the difference between love and lust. Lust was a madness that hit you like a hurricane, a guaranteed wrecker.

'And what was the urgency about that?' Saul demanded as she put down the phone. She said,

'Sorry, but suddenly I thought I might not catch him if I left it any longer. I don't suppose you'd understand.'

'True love?' His grin was devilish. 'Too right I wouldn't. I must take after my mother, half the time I can't remember their names.' That was the most callous, chauvinistic thing Charlotte had ever heard. 'Going to stick with you, is he,' he asked, 'now you're no longer the well-heeled Miss Dunscombe?'

She would have hit him if she had had anything in her hand hard enough to knock him over, but he would probably return a slap across the face, so she gritted her teeth and said sweetly, 'Well, in your case I can understand that it's the money they're after.'

He laughed. 'Not entirely.' Sheer animal magnetism emanated from him like an aura, but she would never show that she was susceptible to it and she said coldly, 'Jeremy would love me if I didn't have a penny.'

'Which you don't.'

'So all *right*, I *know*!' He didn't have to be so boorish. So she had shot out of the room, where she was having a discussion with him, to ring Jeremy and talk about nothing in particular. But that had only taken a couple of minutes. He didn't have to insult her by suggesting that Jeremy only cared about money. 'You don't have to keep reminding me,' she snapped. 'I do know I'm broke. And I know that if we stay under your roof I'll owe you—but just don't expect payment in kind!'

The fringe of hair she was still wearing over her forehead was getting in her eyes and she tossed her head and glared at him and he drawled, 'Your father isn't the only one with inflated ideas about your sex rating. You're not going to be raped—at least not by me.'

She breathed deep, getting enough breath to shriek at him, and the middle button on her blouse popped open and he laughed, 'Although if you go around looking like that I wonder you've avoided it so far.'

Aunt Lucy came into the hall and stopped dead, seeing Charlotte, dishevelled and indignant, then came rushing up demanding, 'What have you been doing to her?'

'That's what you asked me a couple of days ago,' said Saul wearily, 'and the answer's still the same, not a bloody thing.'

'We've been arguing,' said Charlotte. 'I shouldn't be making phone calls while he's talking to me.'

Aunt Lucy had thought he was propositioning her at least. This explanation for Charlotte's flushed face nonplussed her, and there was the blouse. She said sharply,

'You've got a button undone, I told you that blouse was too tight.'

'It wasn't till it shrank in the wash,' Charlotte muttered, 'and it won't be now when I get time to put another stitch in the buttonhole.'

'Do you think we might get down to business?' said Saul.

'Oh, I am so sorry,' said Charlotte. 'Here I go again, nattering on. Just what business did you have in mind?'

'Turning your assets into capital,' he said. 'And I'm referring to the furniture.'

Her defiance drained away, because this was a bitter business. Saul Laurenson put a hand on the hall table, a pretty little Georgian piece that he could have smashed with a clenched fist, and said, 'For instance, this is mine. You'd better see the bills of sale, then you'll know what to get valued. If you wish to sell any of the remaining items perhaps you'd give me first refusal.'

Then the house could stay as it was, looking the same but never the same again. Charlotte had to gulp away the lump in her throat before she could say, 'That could be very convenient.' Aunt Lucy was rubbing the table's edge, where Saul had fingerprinted the patina of the rosewood, with her apron, and Charlotte knew that she was beginning to realise what all this meant. She loved even the furniture here. She had spent most of her life caring for it, as well as for the people who lived in the house.

'Which rooms do you want?' Charlotte asked. They had to get all this settled, and Saul answered promptly, 'I'll keep the bedroom I'm using, and I shall need an office. Your father won't be using his for a while'—if ever—'so I'll stay with that, and perhaps we could share the dining and drawing rooms.'

That should be bearable for a few weeks in the year, and the rest of the time would be like old times. Except that Saul Laurenson would have the right, at any time of the day or night, to march in and start ordering them all around. Charlotte said quietly, 'That sounds reasonable,' and Aunt Lucy said, 'Mr Colin will have to have a room downstairs,' as though they had forgotten that.

'The garden room.' Charlotte had already decided that would be perfect. It was on the ground floor, overlooking the garden and adjacent to the cloakroom. They could turn it into a cosy bed-sitter until her father was fit to climb the stairs again to his old bedroom. 'Is there anything else?' She looked at Saul, who asked, 'May I borrow your horse?'

'To ride?' Of course to ride, he wasn't likely to be setting Kelly to work. She said, 'Of course,' before he could answer, adding, 'Don't ride him hard, he's got a soft mouth.'

If Kelly was ill-treated she couldn't endure that, but Saul's smile was quite different this time. 'I won't jump him over any hedges without checking that the road's clear.' Charlotte smiled faintly in response, sorry she had said that because she was sure he would never ill-treat an animal. Humans maybe. Georgy hardly seemed to mind him around at all, but Aunt Lucy was looking apprehensive, and Charlotte knew that seeing Saul lay a hand on the hall table had made their situation more real to her than Charlotte trying to explain it in the kitchen just now.

'I'm expecting Roger Fairley some time this afternoon,' said Saul. 'If he should turn up before I'm back would you ask him to wait?'

'Yessir,' cracked Charlotte, and he grinned the nice grin again, and said, 'And fasten that button before he gets here. He's a married man with two children, you wouldn't want to upset that.'

She buttoned up hastily. 'I think I'll change,' she said.

'You can't trust anything these days. Hand wash, it said, and see what happens!'

He laughed and went out laughing and Aunt Lucy sighed, 'I don't know what to make of him, I can't make him out.'

'I don't suppose there are many who can,' murmured Charlotte.

'And who's Roger Fairley?'

'The new manager at Dunscombes.' Aunt Lucy gave a little wail of protest and went back into the kitchen shaking her head.

Roger Fairley should know Saul Laurenson better than most, and if Charlotte got the chance she would have a talk with him while he was waiting for Saul. She changed into a high-necked shirt, with secure buttons and a thin velvet-string bow, and brushed her hair into deep shining waves, fastening it back. She was not out to look seductive, just neat and tidy and attractive, so that Roger Fairley would sit and talk, relaxed and communicative.

Maudie had been cleaning the bath when Charlotte passed the open door of the bathroom, and from her expression when she looked up Charlotte knew that she had heard the scene down in the hall. Charlotte gave a wry outsized shrug and Maudie gave a sympathetic grimace. Maudie *was* sympathetic, she liked the Dunscombes, father and daughter, no side on either of them. But she had been fascinated to hear that the tall dark super-looking man owned nearly everything, and him telling Charlotte that her young man wouldn't be wanting her now and talking of *rape*!

Terrible, it was! Maudie couldn't wait to finish her chores so that she could tell her friends and neighbours all about it.

Charlotte phoned back some of the friends who had rung while she was out, and ate a ham sandwich that

Aunt Lucy thrust on her, and when she heard the car draw up she opened the front door and smiled at Roger Fairley.

He had brought his briefcase with him. He looked the kind of young man who rarely made a move without a briefcase, dapper and sharp. She told him that Saul would be back any time; and she was afraid he would, before she had had a chance to get Mr Fairley talking. She led the way into the drawing room and offered a drink, and Mr Fairley said that coffee would be mighty welcome.

Over coffee Charlotte said, 'I'm glad the change of management went off so smoothly this morning. It was an ordeal for all of them because nobody had any idea what to expect.' She enquired how the rest of the day had gone, and listened to the plans with genuine interest, because although she and her father had done with Dunscombes she still cared about its future.

Then she brought in Saul's name. 'Saul's good at the sweet-talk, isn't he? He was very impressive this morning.' She had meant to sound quite admiring, but perhaps she didn't, because Roger Fairley's blue eyes narrowed, although he agreed with her.

'Yes, ma'am, he can be very impressive with the sweet-talk.' Then he added, 'But if he hadn't carried them with him at that little get-together they'd have seen how tough he can be.' He helped himself to another spoonful of sugar, and stirred his coffee slowly, and Charlotte wondered if he was warning her and said bluntly,

'You don't like him?'

He wasn't going to admit disliking his employer, but she thought she had the picture until his face lit with an almost boyish enthusiasm and he said, 'Of course I like him. He wouldn't have got where he is if he hadn't been tougher than hell, but he's the best of bosses and the best of friends.'

'And the worst of enemies?' A man who had forged ahead as Saul Laurenson had must have made enemies, and must have made short work of them too, and Roger Fairley admitted it. 'I reckon so.'

'How did he get where he is?' asked Charlotte. 'All I know is that he went to Australia fifteen years ago. I didn't know him then, but I know that's how it was. And then he turns up as a tycoon. Do tell me what happened in the meantime.'

She settled herself in her chair, looking bright-eyed as a child waiting for a bedtime story. Of course Roger Fairley wasn't going to tell her anything confidential, but he was willing enough to talk; although he might have wondered why she hadn't asked Saul. Or her father, who must have known all this.

He began, 'Well, he had luck from the beginning. He bought this spread in the Australian outback, small by the standards out there, about eight hundred square miles, a cattle station on the route into Queensland. He was making a good thing of it too, but then a mining prospector found bauxite on his land.' She looked blank and he explained, 'The ore that makes aluminium. It was a rich deposit, millions of tons. It got him a seat on the board of Arras Alloys where the big money is, and from then on everything else that he touched prospered.'

'I wonder why,' she murmured. Some men were born lucky, but you did wonder what kind of chemistry made the winners.

Roger Fairley grinned.

'He's a human dynamo—never tired, and they don't come any smarter. And he's afraid of nothing. Your S.A.S. have got a motto that could have been written for him, "Who Dares Wins". I've been working for him for just over five years now and I've seen him take risks and make decisions, without hesitating, that other men would have worried about for months. And I've never known him make the wrong move.'

Obviously Roger Fairley admired Saul Laurenson, and while he was in full flood Charlotte slipped in a personal question. 'He's never married?'

'No. Always crowds of them around, but he says he's never met a girl he's scared of losing.' She could believe that. She asked, 'Are you bringing your wife and children over?' He was, as soon as possible, and she said that when the Fairley family arrived she would love to meet them, so he produced a wad of snapshots from his wallet.

Charlotte couldn't resist snapshots. She joined him on the sofa and he showed her his children, 'Kay and Richie, dressing the tree last Christmas,' and Pamela, his lovely willowy blonde wife. He was proud of them, and Charlotte took snap after snap from him, while he told her where each was taken, and what was going on at the time, until she began to feel that she knew quite a lot about the Fairleys.

She would have loved a peep at any photographs in Saul's wallet, but she couldn't see that coming about, and she doubted if he carried any. If he missed no one he wasn't going to bother with photographs.

He walked in on them while Roger was telling Charlotte about a barbecue party, and showing her Richie in striped apron and cook's hat. It was the last snapshot, and she handed them back with a smile and a 'Thank you,' and asked Saul if he had enjoyed his ride.

'Very much,' he said.

She could imagine him on that cattle station when he first left England. He had changed into an open-necked shirt and cord trousers, and she could imagine him looking much the same as he did now, riding for miles through the scrublands of the vast and lonely outback. Then returning to what kind of home? And who would be waiting there? She had never been so curious about any other man, but then his was an exceptional sort of life and he was altogether an exceptional character.

She got to her feet. 'I'll go and see to Kelly.'

'I've rubbed him down,' said Saul. 'You've got a good horse there.'

'Not for sale,' she said quickly.

'I should hope not,' he said. Roger Fairley was putting his wallet back into his jacket pocket, and picking up his briefcase, and the two men went off into the office.

The next ten days were centred on the hospital where her father was recovering from his heart attack. She visited twice daily, with the best medicine she could offer, constant reassurance that everything was in hand at home. At first it was just a case of sitting beside him, so that when he opened his eyes she was there. But soon he wanted news and then she told him snippets of gossip and passed on messages from friends, and if Saul was with her that always cheered him. He was more than content to accept Saul's offer of indefinite hospitality in what had been the family home, ready to let him buy any of the contents he fancied.

On average Saul went along with her one visit in three days. The rest of the time he was out of the house, perhaps on business, perhaps socially. He had breakfast in the breakfast room, apart from that he ate out, and Charlotte asked no questions because it was none of her business. But seeing him always did her father good. He was still nourishing the crazy notion that Saul was going to look after Charlotte for the rest of her life, and he would have to be stronger before he could accept that the only one looking out for Charlotte was Charlotte.

The nurses knew her by now. Colin Dunscombe, with his handsome looks and his gentlemanly air, was one of their favourite patients, but when Saul arrived with Charlotte even the starchiest of them turned girlish and giggly. The other men in the ward looked forward to seeing Charlotte, and Saul usually walked in with a hand under her elbow.

In the beginning Charlotte had found herself edging away from his touch, but she soon got over that, and it was no act that she was grateful to him. He was keeping a roof over their heads, and seeing them both together was helping her father on his road to recovery. But the closeness was play-acting, and on the way home, a few days before he was due for discharge, she said, 'I hope we're not overdoing it. He's going to be let down if he thinks this is the future settled.'

'The immediate future is,' said Saul. 'In a month or two he'll be up to facing facts. In the meantime let him believe what he wants to believe.'

'Yes—well, thanks, I'm grateful.' She bit her lip and hoped Saul was right, as usual. 'But I think he's blotted Jeremy out. He never mentions him at all. I don't think he remembers I said I was going to marry him.'

'Does Jeremy?' said Saul, and she hunched down in her seat, turning away from him.

'Oh yes,' she said. 'No second thoughts about that. That's what we talk about all the time.'

She wasn't seeing Jeremy so much these days, she wasn't seeing much of anybody except her father, but they did meet occasionally in the afternoons, and after she had visited the hospital and he was through with the evening performance he sometimes drove over. He didn't come to the house. Charlotte didn't want him bumping into Saul, nor into Aunt Lucy, so he would park in the lane and walk across the fields to the patio, and she would stroll down there, sometimes with Tria and Wilbur. She didn't take Georgy to meet Jeremy because Georgy still yapped when Jeremy appeared. But it was warm summer weather, and with Jeremy's arms around her for a little while she could feel almost carefree again.

As soon as they said goodbye, and she walked back to the house, her troubles came to meet her. This was limbo-time. She couldn't really get down to anything until her father came out of hospital. Then she could start work, and begin living a normal if altered life. And it would all be easier when Saul had left.

Sharing the house with him was a perpetual trial. The togetherness they assumed for her father's benefit didn't operate outside the hospital. There hadn't been any more big clashes, but Charlotte always felt on edge when Saul was in the same room, although he always kept his distance.

She knew that the neighbours were talking. Some of them asked her outright what the situation was, and she told them. Most of the financial details were common knowledge anyway. It was what was going on between Saul Laurenson and Charlotte that intrigued them, and the answer to that was, 'Nothing.'

Yes, he owned the firm and he was buying the house, and yes, Charlotte and her father and Aunt Lucy would still be living here, so he would be their landlord. It was a simple straightforward business arrangement. Aunt Lucy seconded that quite fiercely, more concerned for Charlotte's reputation than Charlotte was herself.

Saul was out most evenings, but sometimes he came into the drawing room where Charlotte and Aunt Lucy were sitting. Aunt Lucy was still watching his every move, presumably in case he pounced on Charlotte; and that embarrassed Charlotte as much as it obviously amused Saul. But he could make them both laugh and he could keep them both listening. They got the news from Dunscombes from him. Charlotte hadn't been back there again, although most days some member of the staff phoned to ask how her father was.

Saul told them, 'Roger's been approached by Benjy Hale, who wonders if you're going to carry on designing. He says some of your patterns were best-sellers.'

'In a small way,' said Charlotte. 'But Benjy was a fan of mine.'

'Roger wondered why he turned the colour of beetroot every time he said your name,' said Saul. 'Are you still designing?'

'No.' The break had been made for her, she couldn't go back. 'Anyway,' she said, 'I've got another job lined up.' Saul didn't argue, so he couldn't have thought much of her talents as a designer, and she picked up the book beside her and began to read and hoped it would look as though *she* was closing the subject.

Aunt Lucy had been watching a quiz on television. She went on watching it and Saul opened the *Financial Times* while Charlotte read doggedly on. Poems—she loved poetry. Usually the music of the words in her mind relaxed her, but when Saul was near there was always this tension in her spine making her concentration waver.

'I wonder by my troth what thou and I did till we loved——' she read, and although she knew the lines by heart tonight their meaning seemed fresh and new. She thought, loving someone could become the meaning of your life, the reason for being so that everything else that happened to you was a spin-off.

'What's the book?' Saul asked, and she frowned.

'Poetry.'

'No need to sound so defensive.' She bet he thought poetry was a waste of time, she bet he didn't spend much time reading it, and she nodded towards his paper.

'How are the stocks and shares?'

'Doing nicely, thank you.'

'But of course. Do you believe in the law of averages?' He waited, one eyebrow raised, and she went on, 'Because going by that you're going to start losing before long. Nobody wins for ever. Doesn't that frighten you?'

'You know,' he said gravely, 'it keeps me awake at nights.' No, it didn't. He never considered it. He believed he shaped his own destiny, and Charlotte thought he did too and she resented what seemed to be his effortless success.

I do not have a nice nature, she thought, because I would dearly love to see you fall off your high horse, and a few cracks appearing in that self-sufficiency that Roger Fairley admires so much.

'I'm going to make myself a cup of cocoa,' Aunt Lucy announced. 'Can I get either of you a drink?'

Saul poured himself a whisky, Charlotte said she would settle for cocoa, and as Aunt Lucy went to prepare it Saul looked up from his glass and asked, 'What is this job you've found yourself?'

'It's in a gift shop.' Charlotte had never worked in a shop, but Monique Morris, the owner, was a friend who knew that Charlotte could be relied on to look stunning and was a likeable girl. Whether she would stay smiling, if her feet hurt and customers turned awkward, remained to be seen; but Monique was ready to take her on a trial month, starting whenever she chose. The salary wasn't high, but it was the best offer Charlotte had had.

Another friend, who ran a riding school, would have welcomed her down at the stables but couldn't afford another wage, and that was the general situation. 'And I'm working in a bar on Saturday nights,' she added. 'At the Stage Door in Chipping Queanton.'

'I hope you can stand the pace,' he drawled, and she said briefly,

'I'll have to. Somebody's got to bring home the bacon.'

In fact she was looking forward to starting both jobs. It would be money coming in and it would leave her no time to brood. With the nurse and Aunt Lucy looking after her father everything ought to work out. She was determined on one thing. She wasn't limping home beaten no matter what happened, having Saul Laurenson telling her again that she was spoiled and gutless.

'You'll be able to keep an eye on your fiancé,' he said, sipping the whisky as though he was savouring it. The Stage Door was the pub that the theatre crowd used, very near the theatre, and of course she would be seeing Jeremy there on Saturday evenings; he had put in a word for her, helping her to get the job. She said coldly, 'I don't need to keep an eye on him. We trust each other, we're enough for each other. I suppose you're still seeing my old pal Jo-Ann?' Jo-Ann phoned through here, leaving messages for Saul, but Charlotte wouldn't have brought it up if he hadn't made that crack about Jeremy.

She went on, 'Now there *is* a girl a man would have to keep an eye on, she's always played the field. Still, as you have too that makes you a pair, doesn't it? And as you're so filthy rich you've got to be the one she's been looking for since she was sixteen.'

She was surprised at her own bitchiness, because she wasn't joking. She was angry, although she laughed. Saul must have touched a raw nerve, saying that about Jeremy, and she went to help Aunt Lucy heat the milk for the cocoa, and drank hers in the kitchen.

The day her father was due out of hospital the weather broke. It didn't really matter, he wasn't going to be out in it, but it would have been pleasant if he could have come home in sunshine. They had brought a single bed down into the garden room, which was actually a parlour, part of the house, not an annexe, and everything was comfortable and welcoming.

Nurse Betty Smith, who had looked in the previous day, had declared herself more than satisfied; and with her own bedroom upstairs, linked to an alarm buzzer beside her patient's bed.

Nurse Betty was a small bird-like woman, recommended by Dr Buckston, and Charlotte had ventured, hesitantly, 'He's quite a big man and he may need lifting. Are you—I mean, you can't weigh more than eight stone yourself.'

'Eight six,' Nurse Betty had chirped. 'And my last patient was fourteen stone.' Her eyes fell on Aunt Lucy, and Charlotte's lips twitched because Nurse Betty looked ready to prove her powers of leverage by hoisting Aunt Lucy off the ground.

Fortunately she didn't, and they later took a glass of sherry together and Aunt Lucy declared that she seemed a nice sensible body.

Next morning the nurse went with Charlotte and Saul to bring Colin Dunscombe home. He walked from the car leaning on Charlotte's arm. She had taken along a wheelchair in the boot of the car, but he waved that away and made a slow and steady progress to the end of the hall and the room that was waiting for him.

Charlotte was happy. The worries were still waiting, but her father was back and it was as though the sun was shining for the first time in days. In fact it was raining for the first time in days, but she went singing about the house, her spirits buoyant.

Jeremy rang and she told him the journey from the hospital had been fine. 'He has to rest, of course, that's the thing, and Nurse Betty's on guard and I keep putting my head in and giving him a grin, and he's grinning back, and it's going to be all right, it really is.' She gave a big happy sigh. 'Shall I see you tonight?'

'Sure,' said Jeremy, 'if you want to.'

'Oh, I want!'

He laughed, 'Right, then. Same place, same time?'

'The patio? And why not?'

'I love you,' he said, and she carolled, 'And I love you.'

Putting down the phone, she ran up the stairs. Georgy had been fastened in her bedroom, to keep him from coming across Nurse Betty Smith and having a canine nervous breakdown, but now perhaps he could be transferred to the kitchen. At the top of the stairs Charlotte collided with Saul and beamed on him and said, 'Isn't it a beautiful day?' He looked at a window on which the rain was pattering and she grinned, 'Well, the gardens need it. Anyhow, it isn't going to last. We'll have the sun shining again in no time.'

'No, we won't,' he said, 'we're in for a storm.' Literally speaking he was probably right because, in spite of the rain, the air was heavy. But Charlotte felt suddenly apprehensive, as though his words had a double meaning, carrying a threat. She shrugged and went on her way into the bedroom to fetch Georgy, but she had stopped singing . . .

Charlotte spent the evening with her father. Nurse Betty spent it with Aunt Lucy, and Charlotte and her father had their meal alone. Aunt Lucy produced a dainty tray and, although he had little appetite, Colin Dunscombe emptied the bowl of soup and said how good it was to be back to home cooking.

Charlotte wasn't hungry either. Her father was home again and that was wonderful, but she was wondering now how long she could keep up the pretence that she and Saul had a special understanding, or indeed any understanding at all. It was one thing to walk arm in arm into a hospital ward, and a very different matter pretending, from morning till night, that they were close, when the distance between them was wide and unbridgeable.

Saul wasn't here now. He had gone off in his car late in the afternoon, and when her father asked where he was Charlotte had replied automatically, 'I wouldn't know,' then smiled and said, 'Business, probably.'

Probably off to meet Jo-Ann, she thought. Or somebody else, I wouldn't know; and she promised herself that very soon she was going to tell her father the truth.

They listened to his favourite music, playing quietly. The nurse helped him into bed just after eight o'clock but said it was all right, Charlotte could stay until he was ready to go to sleep. So she curled up in an armchair and to a background of muted Brahms they sometimes talked, sometimes were silent. Nothing was said that might have disturbed him, she watched that, it was all soothing stuff.

She closed her eyes and heard herself sigh softly, and wondered how long it would be before she would dare to say Jeremy's name, and why she should feel so alone when she would be running to meet him in a few hours' time.

Jeremy wouldn't let her down, he *did* love her. It was Saul's cynicism that sometimes put doubts into her mind. Saul didn't believe in love. Saul didn't believe in anything, except taking what you wanted and paying for it, and wouldn't that be lovely for Jo-Ann, who had always believed in settling for the highest bidder?

'Hello,' said her father, as Saul walked in, and Charlotte's heart jerked with a real physical pain for a moment. Sexual electricity, that's what it was. He gave her pins and needles, and she uncoiled from the chair and sat bolt upright.

He smiled at her father, then at her. 'Hello, darling,' he said to her, and stroked her hair lightly. It was a casual gesture, but it carried a suggestion of intimacy that she resented, although it was for her father's benefit. She wanted to ask, 'Did you and whoever she was decide on an early night?' Instead she tried to smile, and found she was smoothing her hair down with both hands as though he had tousled it into wild disorder.

After Saul came her father brightened up. The men talked for a while about Dunscombes' future, while Charlotte watched closely for any sign of distress, but Colin Dunscombe seemed to be finding this reassuring. And the house situation, that was going through the lawyers. And the furniture, Charlotte would get in a valuer. He hadn't discussed any of this with Charlotte since he came home, but now she said quietly, 'Oh yes, I'll be doing that.'

She had been shocked when Saul produced the bills of sale a few days ago to realise how much had already changed hands, on the valuation of his adviser. She would be choosing the expert who came along next time.

'Another thing I've been wondering,' said Colin Dunscombe. 'The nurse, how is her salary being paid?' He was asking Saul, and Charlotte said abruptly,

'I sold my pearls.' They had been an eighteenth birthday present and she had taken them to a retail jeweller friend who had given her a generous price, but a shadow fell on her father's face, so she said, 'Maybe I'll buy them back some time. If not, so what, you can't eat a string of pearls.' Then she took a deep breath. 'Do we still have the other jewellery? The family heirlooms? Mother's aquamarine collar?'

Ever since she knew they were bankrupt she had been afraid to ask that because, of all their possessions, she would have liked to keep some of the jewellery that her mother and grandmother and great-grandmother had worn. Her father shook his head, and when she looked at Saul he shook his head too, disclaiming involvement, so she said inanely, 'Ah well, easy come, easy go.'

A little later she left the men. It was coming up to Aunt Lucy's bedtime and Charlotte sat chatting to Nurse Betty until it was time for the nurse to settle her patient for the night.

Then Charlotte went up to her own room. Eleven o'clock was the time that Jeremy came. That allowed for last-minute delays after the evening performance finished, and gave him time to drive from Chipping Queanton. He hadn't phoned, so he was coming, although it was a wretched night.

There was always the summerhouse to provide a little shelter from the rain, but sitting here, watching the minutes tick by, meeting Jeremy in secret like this suddenly seemed ridiculous. Her father wasn't going to be wandering around, so tonight she was bringing Jeremy into the house. Not upstairs, she didn't want to give Aunt Lucy palpitations, but into the drawing room.

Considering she had been so full of sweetness this morning her mood now was surprisingly aggressive. She hardly recognised herself these days, but if Saul was downstairs she would say, 'Just off to meet my lover. Don't lock up, I'm bringing him back.' The only way she could have described her mood was 'spoiling for a fight', and that wasn't like her at all.

She was quite disappointed to find the ground floor in darkness, and when she stepped outside she hesitated about going back into the house to find a torch because it was pitch black out here. Instead she stood for a minute, waiting for her eyes to acclimatise.

It was raining too, a few heavy drops that could be the end or the beginning of a downpour, but the cool air was welcome, and the rain on her face was refreshing. She walked slowly at first across the lawns, but as soon as she could see where she was going the trees took shape and she quickened her step so that she was almost running when she reached the patio.

Jeremy was waiting. A tall dark shadow, out here in the rain, not even in the shelter, and Charlotte ran full tilt into his arms. 'Oh, bless you,' she whispered, eyes closed, face pressed against him, 'I don't know what I'd have done if you hadn't come. Oh, love, do I need you! Oh, it's been——' He stopped her mouth with a kiss and all her frustration and anger melted, and it was such bliss that she could have stood like this for ever. But when the kiss deepened her senses quickened. Jeremy had never kissed her this way before, sending such sensations through every nerve that her whole body clamoured, kissing her as though he would kiss the life out of her. She was on fire, and her fingers tightened in his hair, clinging to him, wrapping him in her flame.

The hair was wrong. The wrong texture. Jeremy's hair was fine and silky, and this was not Jeremy, and she jerked back and yelped, 'Let go of me!'

It was Saul, of course. She had taken it for granted he was Jeremy, this place and this time. She hadn't stopped to check, she had just run to him. She shrieked, 'I thought you were Jeremy! He should have been here. What are you doing here?'

Rain was pouring down. The heavens must have opened in the last couple of minutes, but she hadn't noticed till now that water was streaming over her like a waterfall. She gulped and gasped, 'You had no right to do that!'

'When a woman throws herself at me I reckon that gives me the right,' and she knew he was laughing although she could hardly see him for rage and rain.

'I thought you were Jeremy.' He must know that. He must have been strolling out here, she supposed, and the filthy weather had stopped Jeremy coming, but Saul knew she would never have flung herself into *his* arms.

He drawled, 'In no way am I Jeremy, but if you're

that desperate I could act as stand-in.' The terrifying
thing was that Jeremy's kisses had never got to her like
that kiss, and she spat,

'You're revolting!'

'And I thought I was being obliging.'

He laughed then and she backed away, nearly stumbl-
ing over the stone hound, making a dash for the house. In
her bedroom she stripped off her wet clothes and rubbed
her hair furiously, beside herself with righteous anger. And
scared sick, because she had had the narrowest of escapes.
She could so easily have let him make love to her, right
out there in the rain on the patio. Only a hair's breadth
had saved her, and now her self-disgust was torturing her,
so that she crept downstairs and poured herself a very stiff
whisky, and got it down, coughing and choking, and let it
blot out everything and drug her to sleep . . .

She woke with the suggestion of a thick head, but by
daylight the confusion of the night seemed less traumatic.
That's what it had been, a confusion, a mix-up. A genuine
mistake on her part, although Saul had been ready
enough to take advantage of it, and she would be ice cold
when she saw him again. He would never get near enough
to touch her again, because he was such an expert lover
that he was lethal. All that practice with all those girls
whose names he couldn't remember, and he wasn't adding
her to their number.

She was downstairs early, but Saul had already left the
house, and she spent the morning helping her father
answer personal mail that had been arriving for him. After
lunch she went along to the shop, where she would be
starting work next week, and checked that the offer still
stood. Then, on impulse, she decided to call on Jeremy.

As the weather worsened he had probably decided
against an open-air rendezvous last night, and who could
blame him? Or something had turned up, something con-

nected with work, probably. She would have phoned him later in the day but, with an hour or two to spare, she parked as near as she could to his flat.

The door opening on the road was ajar and she went up the stairs. She tapped on the flat door and it swung inwards and she called, 'Anybody in?' as she walked in.

The living room was empty. 'Hello!' she called, and from the bedroom came the sound of a scuffle, and giggles. Peter must have somebody in there. She had picked the wrong time to come calling, so she croaked, 'Sorry,' and turned to creep away.

'Go *on*, answer her!' the girl's voice was shrill. 'If you don't open that door I will!' and Charlotte froze, staring at the door, and then it opened and Jeremy stood there, barelegged in a dressing gown.

Behind him was a flash of bright red hair and a pasty-pale face. Lesley! Lesley and *Jeremy*! His mouth opened and closed and Charlotte heard herself say, 'I know, you're rehearsing her lines with her.' She addressed herself to Lesley. 'He told me how you're always forgetting your lines—well, this should be quite a performance.'

Then, somehow, she got out of the room and down the stairs and along the street to where her car was parked. She sat in the car for a little while, waiting for delayed shock to strike and her hands to start shaking. But it didn't. It would, of course, but now she still felt strangely calm.

Saul was right again. Saul, who never made a mistake, had said that with all the money gone Jeremy could stop loving her; but Saul wasn't going to know that for sure. She was going to hang on to the few tatters of pride she had left.

The heartache of losing Jeremy would come, and it would hurt dreadfully, but her immediate concern just now was a desperate determination to stop Saul knowing or guessing what she had just seen.

CHAPTER EIGHT

THE phone was ringing when Charlotte walked into the hall and as she picked it up Jeremy said, 'Hello? Charlotte?'

'Nice timing,' she said.

'Look, please, let me explain.'

'I wish I could.' She couldn't bear the sound of his voice, and she went on talking over it. 'I'm sure it would be fascinating, but I really am pressed for time and I really don't care.'

Then she put down the phone and looked at her hand, resting on it, and the shaking was starting. Explain, he'd said! How could he explain what she'd just seen? Anger was making her shake, although perhaps she was being a hypocrite because last night she had been in Saul's arms. But that was different, that was a mistake. As soon as Saul had kissed her she had known and she had stopped it right away. Well, almost right away.

Even the memory made her heart lurch, and she mustn't think about Saul. Nor about Jeremy. She must get busy and keep busy. She looked in on her father, who was resting, with Nurse Betty sitting by the window knitting an emerald green sweater. Then she went into the kitchen where Aunt Lucy was cleaning the silver, and had everything spread out on a newspaper on the kitchen table. 'All right, was it?' Aunt Lucy enquired.

She was referring to Charlotte's job. 'I start on Monday,' said Charlotte. That was all right, although very little else was. If Aunt Lucy knew what had just happened she would be appalled, and of course she wasn't going to know.

'One thing I meant to do and didn't,' said Charlotte, 'was go into Pugh's and ask if someone would come out and value our furniture. What there is left of it.'

Aunt Lucy had been polishing the silver teapot. 'We're not letting this go,' she announced, clutching it. 'I haven't cleaned this every week for the last forty years to hand it over to somebody else. Mr Laurenson will be owning us lock, stock and barrel at this rate.'

Charlotte tried to grin, 'But not body and soul,' and Aunt Lucy snorted, 'I shouldn't think he's much bothered about souls, but I've been thinking about bedrooms. Where yours is. And I think you and me could do with changing over.'

Charlotte's room was next to the guestroom that had now become Saul's, while Aunt Lucy slept down the other end of the passage, and Charlotte began to laugh. 'You don't really imagine he'll come marching into my room one night?' Aunt Lucy's lips pursed and Charlotte chortled, 'If he did I'd give a lot to see his face if you sat up!'

'I'm not laughing,' said Aunt Lucy, and she was right, it wasn't a laughing matter, because a night might come when Saul couldn't sleep, and if Charlotte should wake and find him near she might not have the strength to send him away. But she could lock her door, and would, although she was not changing rooms because that would be admitting she was scared to sleep near him.

She had to reassure Aunt Lucy with more than the promise of a locked door, so she said, 'I'll tell you something, love. Saul Laurenson doesn't need to put himself out to get all the women he wants, so he isn't going to waste his time trying to nab me. If I get myself involved with him it will be my own fault, and I've trouble enough on my hands.'

She looked down at her hands, on which the aquamarine sparkled, and while Aunt Lucy muttered she changed the subject. 'I might as well sell this too.'

'Your ring?' Aunt Lucy was shocked. 'Oh no, that would spoil the set—the collar and the earrings. Your father got you that to match.'

'They've gone,' said Charlotte. 'All the old jewellery's gone,' and for the moment the fight went out of Lucy Snowe. She slumped in her chair, and her hands, black with metal polish, lay heavy on the table.

'He shouldn't have done that.' She kept shaking her head. 'He shouldn't have got rid of that, he should have kept the collar for you. Has Mr Laurenson got that as well?'

'Saul didn't buy them,' said Charlotte. 'I don't know where they went, and it's no use fretting.'

'*Men!*' Lucy Snowe pulled herself together, picking up the polishing duster again and attacking the teapot. 'When Mr Colin's back on his feet I shall have something to say to him!'

Charlotte chuckled, 'Watch you don't give him a relapse!'

'A fine birthday you're going to have this year!' The aquamarine ring had been a birthday present. Charlotte's next birthday was less than two weeks away, and it would be very different from the celebrations of previous years.

'With luck,' she said, 'we'll have a few things straightened out by then,' and she went into the hall to ring Benedict Pugh, dealer in fine arts and antiques.

Mr Pugh's shop was a few doors from Dunscombes in Chipping Queanton high street, and when Charlotte explained he said he would come out himself, and at once. When he arrived he held her hand longer than necessary, telling her how sorry he was about everything. She extricated herself with a smile. She didn't want to offend him, but she felt he had done enough patting, and she took him into the drawing room and produced Saul's bills of sale and asked if he thought these prices had been reasonable.

Mr Pugh checked pieces and prices and announced, 'Not over-generous, but fair enough.' So her father hadn't been cheated. Except by himself, of course, as his own worst enemy.

'You're wanting to sell some of your other things?' The dealer's acquisitive glance was darting around the room, and Charlotte said,

'I just want them valued, I want you to put a price on them. I do have a buyer who's getting first refusal.'

'A dealer?'

'A friend.'

Like every other local businessman Benedict Pugh knew about Saul Laurenson. 'Yes, of course,' he said.

'Anything he doesn't take,' said Charlotte, 'we'll probably have to sell anyway, so if you're interested——'

That put Mr Pugh in something of a spot. If somebody else was buying he wanted Charlotte to get the best market price, because he always had had a soft spot for her. But if he was buying himself he had to make a profit. In the end he valued at the price he would have asked. If he was offered second refusal he would explain that, or suggest putting the items into his shop and taking a commission on a sale. He was sure that he and Charlotte Dunscombe could come to some arrangement.

He enjoyed going round the house with her, the scent of her hair in his nostrils, brushing against her more or less by accident from time to time. They ended in the drawing room again, and Benedict tore the pages from his notebook and handed them over, and Charlotte thanked him and asked what she owed him.

'That's what friends are for,' he said. 'It's been my pleasure.'

She protested prettily, 'But you're the expert and you've come out here and done all this valuation.' He was of course entitled to a fee, but she had hoped he might waive it, because every penny counted with her these days.

'I won't hear of it,' he assured her.

'That *is* kind of you.'

'Think nothing of it.' He was squeezing her hand again. 'And if there's anything else I can do——'

'Such as what?' asked Saul. 'It's the furniture that's on offer, not the girl.'

He was in that blessed high-backed armchair again, and Benedict dropped her hand like a hot coal. She said, 'I do apologise, Benedict, and I'm very grateful to you,' and went to the front door with him and thanked him again and said she would be in touch.

'I hope you will,' said Benedict, 'any time.' But he looked down the hall before he said it, as though checking that Saul hadn't followed them out, and Charlotte knew that if Saul had appeared Benedict would have made his goodbye very crisp and businesslike.

She went back into the drawing room, demanding, 'What was that all about? Did you have to be so boorish? He was doing me a favour, valuing the furniture for nothing.'

'For nothing?' Saul's tone was derisive. 'You can't be so naïve that you don't know the bargain he had in mind.'

Benedict Pugh was overweight for his height and balding, but his admiration had been a little balm to her pride, reassuring her that when she walked down the street men's eyes followed her. But the memory of Jeremy standing in the doorway of the bedroom, and behind him the swirl of Lesley's red hair, kept coming back and she said savagely, 'Of course I know he fancies me. I'm broke, but I still get whistled at.'

She thrust Benedict's list at Saul. This was the rest of the good pieces. Some time they would have to furnish a small home of their own, but she was only keeping the basics for that. She said, 'He's a friend, but I'm sure he hasn't let that influence the prices.'

Saul totted up the figures in his head, running his finger down the pages, and she knew he would reach the right answer as sure as a calculator. Then he took out a cheque-book and wrote a cheque.

Charlotte felt hollow. It was done so quickly, like set-tling a grocery account, and that one signature meant that from now on almost everything here belonged to Saul. Roger Fairley had said he made quick decisions, so she asked, 'Don't you want to check for woodworm or anything?'

'Bound to be some,' he said, 'but nothing's falling apart.'

Except me, she thought. She put a hand over her mouth, looking at the cheque: date, figure, signature, of course it was all correct. She opened the little walnut davenport, which Benedict had valued at two hundred and fifty pounds, then asked, 'May I?'

'Of course,' said Saul, and she put the cheque in the top drawer.

She needed to do something energetic. If she stood around, staring about her, she was going to burst into tears. What a day! she thought. I lose the man who said he loved me and all the things I've lived with all my life. She went out into the garden to find something to do that would exhaust her, the lawns needed mowing for a start. Yesterday's rain and today's dewy-damp atmosphere had revived them remarkably.

Old Tom was putting away his tools in one of the out-houses. 'I've come for the mower,' she said, and he warned her, 'Don't get overdoing it,' as he did every time

Charlotte pitched into the heavier work. 'Mr Pugh's been calling, then,' said Tom. 'What was he wanting?'

According to Saul, me, thought Charlotte, and the sui-cidal way I feel right now if he'd asked me out tonight I'd have accepted. She said, 'He came to value some of the furniture. Mr Laurenson's buying it. You know he's buying the house.' Everybody knew that Saul was buying the house, and Tom nodded, taking his pipe out of his pocket. Half the time there was no tobacco in it, he didn't light it now, just clamped it between his teeth.

'I remember him coming up here,' he said, 'before he went off to Australia.' Aunt Lucy didn't, but the saddles would probably be delivered to the stables. 'I can see it as plain as yesterday,' old Tom went on. 'He was walking up and down, looking up at the house, and I wondered what he was up to—I thought he was a gypsy—and I shouted across what did he want, and he grinned and said, "This'll do." I didn't know what he was talking about, but the way things have turned out it makes you wonder whether he'd got this place marked.'

'With his luck,' said Charlotte bitterly, 'if he had, my father might as well have handed it over to him there and then.'

The mower, a pull-starter, proved sluggish, making her hot and cross before she began. It was nearing the end of summer and the mower needed servicing. She would have to get it to the garage and she would hand the bill to Saul, because surely that came under overheads. It was a fairly heavy machine, capable of pulling her into hedges or over flower beds unless she kept her mind on the job and turned down the throttle in time for turning, and even then it often whirled her round so that it was all she could do to stay on her feet.

She didn't want to give Saul the bill. She didn't want

him paying for anything around here, but she couldn't and her father couldn't, and it was a ridiculous quibble when he had just bought the place lock, stock and barrel.

She could imagine the tall gipsy-like boy Tom saw in the old days walking up and down by the stables, looking up at the house, maybe comparing it with the van he was living in at the time. He had told her when he first came back here that for the last ten years he couldn't recall a single thing he had wanted that he hadn't got; and now he had the house, and of course the business, and she was almost sure he wouldn't mind having her, but not enough to put himself out to get her.

If she ran into his arms, like last night, he'd take her fast enough, but that was never going to happen. Nothing good could come of that, because it would mean no more to him than acquiring another piece of furniture. Less probably, the furniture would keep its value.

She turned up the throttle of the lawnmower and roared up and down the lawn a couple of times, passing Georgy who was lying on the grass under the walnut tree and warning him, 'You'll get rheumatism in your tum lying there.' Passing the tree for the third time the mower spluttered and stopped and Charlotte swore and began the cord-jerking routine all over again. She got a click but no following whirr, and she pulled and panted to no avail until she was gibbering with frustration. 'You great ugly useless thing—shift, can't you?'

'Talking to me?' said Saul.

She hadn't noticed him coming across the grass. She sat down, cross-legged, beside Georgy, and fastened her hair again in the wide tortoiseshell slide that held it back from her face. Tendrils of hair were sticking to her cheeks and forehead, making her skin tickle.

'I never thought I should see you sweating.' Saul sat down too and grinned, and she glared.

'I often do, when I mow the lawns. What did you expect me to do? Glow, like a Victorian lady?'

'Did Victorian ladies mow lawns?'

'Shouldn't think so, in those crinolines. But that was the saying, wasn't it? "Horses sweat, gentlemen feel the heat, and ladies glow".'

He gave her a leer of mock admiration. 'It must be a fine thing to have had that grand education.'

Charlotte had gone to a good school, but she had no doubt that Saul's mind was more cultured than hers, and so far as brain power went she wasn't competing. 'And you were usually top of the class, according to your old school friend,' he reminded her.

That had to be Jo-Ann, and Charlotte knew exactly how she would have said it, because Jo-Ann considered intelligence in a girl was not sexy. Low cunning was all right, Jo-Ann had plenty of that, and Charlotte was sure they didn't waste much time talking about her, and just stopped herself from snapping, 'Jo-Ann never came top in anything—but then she always had other things on what passes for her mind.'

She was shocked at the cattiness Jo-Ann was causing in her these days. Jo-Ann had never been one of Charlotte's favourite people, but now the very mention of her name irritated her like prickly heat.

Georgy had rolled over on to his back and Saul was scratching his stomach and Charlotte said, 'I can't make up my mind if he's paralysed with terror, or whether you've done the impossible and he really isn't scared.'

Saul laughed and went on tickling Georgy for a few minutes, then he got up and started the mower. Charlotte clapped her hands, giving him a round of applause although she would have preferred him to have found it just a little harder to get the engine ticking over. 'You'd flooded the carburettor,' he told her.

'How careless of me. Know a lot about machinery, do you?'

'I've tinkered with some in my time.' He took off his jacket and dropped it on the grass. Under it he wore a grey silk shirt. He set off with the lawnmower and Charlotte called after him,

'Jack of all trades?'

'And master of none,' he countered cheerfully, and he could afford to be cheerful because that didn't apply to him. All his talents, so far as Charlotte could see, had paid off, and he was handling the lawnmower very competently too. Coming back, he slowed down when he reached her and said, 'I find that experience is rarely wasted,' and leaned over as though he was going to kiss her but she swayed back against the tree. He kept the engine running. 'Your father could be watching us. Don't you want him to think we're very good friends?'

'I'm not sure that I do,' she said. 'And have you stopped to consider that Aunt Lucy also could be watching?'

'If she is,' said Saul, 'I'm drinking none of her cocoa tonight.'

'You never do.'

'I'm no fool.' He touched the throttle and moved off again. 'She could still have some of those sleeping pills.'

Charlotte got a fit of giggles at the thought of Aunt Lucy doping Saul into sound slumber at nights. She sat chuckling, watching him, and when the chuckles subsided she was still smiling inside as the peace of the evening stole over her. Even the hum of the lawnmower seemed soothing. She pulled Saul's jacket around her shoulders. She wasn't cold, but it would be the easiest thing to catch a chill, sitting here after getting so overheated. Anyhow it felt good, like a light arm around her.

Rooks were wheeling over the tall trees, black against the pearl-grey sky, and she watched the man and the movement of his muscles rippling under the thin silk of his shirt. The mower didn't take him off his feet when he turned it around, it wouldn't have dared, and she smiled when he looked across at her and he smiled, but neither spoke, even when he passed close by, and the silence was strangely healing. Her fingers closed on Saul's jacket, holding it around her, and she felt contentment growing and the misery of the day receding until, for the moment, she was strong and happy again.

He finished the lawns—and a very professional job it was—and came across to her, and she got up and handed him his coat. As she did his wallet fell out and she thought, I could have had a quick peep at that while you were down the far end; and then, My stars, what am I coming to?

She asked, 'Do you carry photographs?'

'No,' he said. 'Why?'

'Roger Fairley showed me his family.'

'Well, I'm sorry I can't. No family and no photos.'

He wasn't sweating from the exercise, his skin looked cool; and she wondered if it felt cool and wanted to touch it, along the hard lines of the cheekbones. 'Where does this go?' asked Saul, hand on the mower, and she said,

'I'll show you.' When it was stacked in the shed she said, 'I'm going to check that Kelly's all right for the night.'

There were three stalls in the stables. Long ago there had been three horses, and a governess cart, but that was before the age of the car. Charlotte remembered her father riding to hounds, but after Prince had died some time ago the only horse in the stables had been hers. Kelly ambled around a field all day, unless Charlotte was riding him, and she was going to have less time for that in the future.

The warm smell of hay filled the air and Kelly nuzzled her shoulder and she said, 'I was thinking of letting him go to the riding school for exercise. Mary Whitehead who runs it is a friend of mine, she'd only let experienced riders near him.'

'I'll exercise him while I'm here,' said Saul.

'All right.' He ran a hand down the horse's gleaming neck and Charlotte said, 'It's a crazy life isn't it? I wonder if we've still got your saddles.'

'One of them.' He looked up to where the tack was hanging on the wall and she said,

'Tom remembers you bringing them. He says you were looking at the house, and when he asked you what you wanted you said, "This'll do." He says it makes him wonder if you'd always planned to come back here and move in.'

Saul grinned, 'Not particularly. I could have said the same about Buckingham Palace.'

She made a small grimace. 'I hope not, as you always get what you want.' She wanted him to hold and kiss her the way he had on the patio, and the longing for him was so strong in her that she felt he must sense it. It had to be like a perfume or a cry. She looked at him and willed him to look back with some of her own desperation, then she would be in his arms. She croaked, 'How does it feel to always be a winner?'

'If you really want to know, bloody hard work,' he said crisply. 'I wasn't born with a silver spoon. I'm earning what I've got and I'd better get back to earning it.'

'Thanks for mowing the lawns,' she said.

'A pleasure.'

He went out of the stables and she closed her eyes and gripped her folded arms until her fingertips ached. She shouldn't have said that. She shouldn't have said anything and then he would have reached for her, she was sure of it. It was tactless to keep on harping about all his achievements being luck. He would have made it if they hadn't found bauxite on his land, working the way he did. No wonder he was beginning to get irritated, and it was positively the last time she would mention luck.

She spent what was left of the evening sorting out her wardrobe. Her life-style had changed drastically, she would have little use now for the high fashion clothes with the couture names, so she was taking them along to one of the nearly-new shops and hoping to turn them into cash.

Her father was asleep, and Aunt Lucy and Nurse Betty had gone to their own bedrooms, when Charlotte got into the bathroom. She washed her hair and showered, and came out into the passage as Saul was walking down, towards the bathroom and her. He grinned at her, 'We'll have to stop meeting like this.'

She laughed, but she was very conscious of his nearness. This was the second naked man in a dressing gown she had encountered today. Jeremy's legs were whiter and thinner. Saul's were tanned and tautly muscled like the rest of his body would be, and from looking down at his legs she looked back down the corridor, because she couldn't quite make herself stare directly at him.

He looked down the corridor too. 'Is Miss Snowe lurking?'

Charlotte gurgled, 'She's rather too wide to make a successful lurker, but she's in two minds whether to move me to the end of the passage, and if there's too much chatting up in bathrobes she will.'

He roared with laughter and she laughed too, and Georgy at Charlotte's heels contributed a few yaps, and Aunt Lucy's door opened and her head popped out. At which Georgy yapped again and the door opposite opened and Nurse Betty's head appeared.

'My God,' exclaimed Saul, 'the house is alive with chaperones!' He bowed to them, 'Goodnight, ladies,' and both heads shot back.

Charlotte went on her way smiling. When she closed her bedroom door after her she hesitated. She had never locked the door in this house in all her life, but earlier today she had thought it might be wise. The key was stiff when she tried to turn it. It might stick, the lock should be oiled and she would do that tomorrow. She decided not to bother tonight because Saul wasn't coming in here, of course he wasn't.

She sat up in bed, in the darkness, and thought of Jeremy. She should have pressed one of the red roses he'd sent her after the car accident, a memento of a dead love, but the petals had fallen and the flowers had gone. She wondered what she would say if he phoned again and a gentle melancholy settled on her, in a silence broken only by Georgy's snores, until she heard footsteps coming down the passage and the floorboard that creaked outside Saul's door, and very softly the sound of his door closing.

Suddenly she was pierced with loneliness. Oh, Jeremy, she thought. All you said, all I thought we meant to each other. The tears came then, and she let them flow in the darkness because there was nobody near her to know or to care.

CHAPTER NINE

HER father was still sleeping on Monday morning when Charlotte left for work. Saul was in the kitchen, drinking coffee and reading the headlines, and Charlotte who had come down earlier and taken a cup of coffee up to her bedroom said to Aunt Lucy, 'I'm off now.'

'You ought to have got up in time for a cooked break-fast,' Aunt Lucy scolded.

'No time this morning. Wish me luck.'

'All the luck in the world,' said Saul, 'but remember——'

Charlotte pulled a face. 'I know, luck is a matter of bloody hard work,' and Lucy Snowe's face registered strong disapproval.

'Sorry,' said Charlotte, 'I seem to be picking up bad habits from somewhere.'

'Or from somebody.' Lucy Snowe glared at Saul, who went on reading his paper.

Charlotte was waiting outside the Gift Box when Monique Morris arrived to open the shop, gave her a cheerful smile and said, 'I've got a hunch you're going to make a super saleswoman.'

'I do hope so,' said Charlotte. She had worn Dunscombe jewellery that had been for sale, but there had been no effort in that. Serving customers in the Gift Box could be a tougher task.

The other assistant walked in while Monique was going through her mail and Charlotte was looking around and trying to memorise the merchandise. Monique was a Junoesque young woman, in a flowing red Indian cotton caftan and jangling bangles and earrings. Tessa Adams was neater, in navy skirt and powder blue blouse, and her greeting for Charlotte was an offhand, 'Oh, hello.'

Tessa was Benjy Hale's girl-friend and she had always resented Charlotte Dunscombe. Although this was a come-down if you like, the Dunscombes losing everything like this, even in jeans Charlotte managed to look like a film star.

It was that hair, Tessa decided, and she said, 'I always wondered, is your hair real? I mean, do you wear a piece?'

Charlotte tugged at the roots and said ruefully, 'It's real all right. I wonder if I could cut it off and flog it.'

'Are you that hard up?'

'Oh yes,' said Charlotte, and Tessa saw the shadows under her eyes as though she hadn't been sleeping, and felt a glimmering of sympathy.

Trade was brisk. The Gift Box was having a ten per cent reduction sale as the season was almost over. But with the sunshine back the town was still crowded, and a continual procession of tourists ambled through the shop.

Monique watched Charlotte and was impressed, because nothing seemed too much trouble for her, and the customers liked that. She had a smile for everybody, and as the morning wore on even Tessa was talking to her. When Monique had first mentioned that Charlotte was coming to work here Tessa had said, 'I can't stand her,' but by lunchtime Tessa was admitting, to herself, that when you got to know her perhaps Charlotte Dunscombe wasn't so bad after all.

Saul walked into the shop just before one o'clock. Tessa was near Charlotte, and as Charlotte gave a little gasp of surprise Tessa opened her eyes wide and asked, 'Who's he?'

'Saul Laurenson,' said Charlotte. He hadn't seen her yet. He was looking around, but she was partly obscured by a trellis partition.

Tessa had heard about Saul Laurenson from Benjy, and everybody knew he was buying the Dunscombe house and staying there. Tessa giggled softly, 'Now I know why you look as though you haven't been sleeping,' and the woman who was buying the photograph frame that Charlotte was wrapping up goggled.

'If I haven't,' muttered Charlotte, 'it's nothing to do with him.' But she hurried across with her heart pounding because the last time Saul had come looking for her he had brought bad news. She asked 'Is anything the matter?' and was relieved when he smiled.

'I've come to take you to lunch,' he said, 'unless you've made other arrangements.'

Her lunch hour was one till two, although she hadn't mentioned that to him, and she said, 'Thanks, I'd like that.' She looked at Monique for permission and Monique said, 'Of course,' very graciously and gave Charlotte a wink and a grin as they walked out.

'Busy morning?' Saul asked, as they went along with the crowds.

'Very busy. Wouldn't you know I'd start on Sales week?'

'The glow suits you.'

'You mean I'm sweating?' She dabbed her warm cheeks with the back of her hand. They were nearing the theatre and she asked, 'Where shall we eat?'

'I thought here,' he said. 'Where you'll be working on Saturday nights,' and he was guiding her through the swing doors of the Stage Door before she could protest, although this was the last place she would have chosen. Even if Jeremy was not here some of his colleagues would be, and she made for a wooden bench in the shadows where she hoped she could pass unnoticed.

Saul acquired a menu which she knew by heart. 'The pâté, please,' she said, 'and half of lager.' The place was almost full of strangers, but she could see Peter propping up the bar with the electrician and assistant producer of the Little Theatre, and she kept her head down and turned away. Through the window, sitting at a table in the garden, she glimpsed Lesley and thought, I can't work here. She would have to give the landlord some excuse because she couldn't stand behind that bar chatting with Jeremy's friends.

When Saul came back, with her pâté and half and a ploughman's and a pint for himself, she told him about her morning, mimicking the customers, making him smile. He sat on the arm of the bench, and the crowds seemed to fade away leaving her and Saul all alone. 'What have you been doing this morning?' she asked him.

'Booking flights,' he said.

'For you?' He nodded, and everything seemed to go quiet. 'When?' she asked.

'A week today.'

'Where are you going?'

'Canada.'

'How long for?' Her voice was so breathless that it might have sounded eager, because he told her, 'You'll have your home to yourself for quite a while.'

'That should please Aunt Lucy.' Charlotte made herself smile, and asked him about his Canadian interests. She listened, but the gaiety had gone out of her and the outside world was rushing in until the noise and crush in here were becoming almost unbearable.

'I'll have to be going,' she said, as the theatre crowd trooped through from the garden, Jeremy among them. He spotted her as she saw him and took a step towards her, then noticed Saul and shrugged and went out of the pub. She gave him a few minutes to get away and then stood up. 'Back to work,' she said. 'Thank you, I enjoyed that.'

All but the last ten minutes! If Saul hadn't been with her Jeremy would have spoken to her and perhaps they could have ended up friends again. Only friends, because she would never again trust him, but of course she had missed him.

She would miss Saul too. A week today and Saul would be gone and her home would be her own again. But he would leave a void. She was astonished to find that, try as she might, she simply could not imagine the house without him.

In a few days Charlotte had settled into the routine of work. Her father's improvement was steady and life was not too bad at all. She was enjoying her job. She brought sandwiches for lunch and ate them in the office, that way there was no risk of bumping into Jeremy. Saul didn't come to take her to lunch again, but Tessa asked if she would like to eat with her and Benjy.

'Benjy's always had a crush on you, you know,' Tessa confided. 'I used to be really jealous of you, I suppose I still am a bit, but you've got Mr Laurenson, haven't you, so you wouldn't be bothering about Benjy.'

'Nobody's got Mr Laurenson,' said Charlotte, 'but I've brought a packed lunch. Another time, maybe?'

Jo-Ann probably thought she had Saul, although Charlotte could have told her that wouldn't last. He was out most nights, he never suggested Charlotte going with him, and from the looks of it he was seeing Jo-Ann, because when she came into the Gift Box on Friday morning she had that sickening simper on her face. She affected surprise, gasping when she saw Charlotte helping a customer, 'You're *never* working here! Well, I know Saul's taken over your father's business, but I didn't realise you were actually going out to work.'

Of course she did. She had only come in to put on an act, and Charlotte said, 'Wasn't I lucky? Jobs don't grow on trees these days.'

'You'll never stick it,' said Jo-Ann.

'Watch me,' said Charlotte, putting the purchase into a bag, ringing up the sale and thanking the customer. 'Now, what can I do for you?'

Jo-Ann bought a scarf in a swirl of colours, one of which was blue, and holding it up to her face she said, 'Blue to match my eyes. Saul says I have the loveliest eyes he's ever seen.'

Charlotte said nothing. Tessa and Monique were occupied and Jo-Ann had Charlotte cornered, which was obviously her objective, because she was almost whispering, 'Folk are saying you and Saul are having an affair because you're living in the same house.'

'Rubbish!' said Charlotte crisply.

She and Saul sparred with words each time they met, mostly cheerfully, sometimes edgily, but she saw little of him; and she kept telling herself that she couldn't wait for next Monday. Then the house would be empty of that electricity he generated. As much thunder as lightning really, making her get up in the night and open windows because he was crowding in on her dreams.

'I know that.' Jo-Ann sounded so smug that Charlotte could have hit her. 'Well, I would know, wouldn't I? You don't get out much since your father came home from hospital, do you?'

Saul had probably told her, although it could have come through somebody else, that Charlotte went home from work and walked the dogs and rode her horse and worked in the house and the garden. She turned down invitations because she didn't want to go out. She just wanted to get good and tired before she fell into bed, because it was at bedtime that she got the miseries. She was still hurt by the easy way Jeremy had given up. He hadn't even tried to phone her again.

'My father hasn't been back a week,' she said, and Jo-Ann asked abruptly,

'What are you doing tomorrow night?'

Charlotte should have been working at the Stage Door, but she had phoned the landlord on Monday night and said she was very sorry but she couldn't take the job after all. Now she murmured, 'Nothing really,' without stopping to think, and Jo-Ann said,

'Come round for a drink, about eight o'clock. Just for a chat, just the two of us.'

There is nothing I would like less, thought Charlotte, than a cosy little chat with you, swapping confidences. She said, 'Thanks, I'll try,' and Jo-Ann said, 'That's a date, I'm relying on you,' and paid for her scarf and went off smiling as though she had the bargain of a lifetime.

It was a date that Charlotte had no intention of keeping. She was dog tired when she got home from work next day, and when she phoned Jo-Ann her excuse was genuine. 'I've just got in and I'm absolutely shattered. Could we make it another night?' But Jo-Anne wailed,

'You *promised*! I've cooked a flan and Mary's coming.'

Mary was an old friend of Charlotte's, an hour or two with her she wouldn't mind, so she said, 'Well, all right. Will you let me put my feet up, and can I come just as I am?'

'Of course you can,' cooed Jo-Ann. 'Come in any old thing.'

So Charlotte stayed in her jeans, changing a limp white shirt for a fresh one, and just before eight o'clock she drew up, in her little red car, outside Jo-Ann's family home, an architect-designed modern bungalow.

There were plenty of cars parked along the road, but none in Jo-Ann's drive. Charlotte rang the bell and Jo-Ann answered, wearing a gold hareem suit that made Charlotte whistle, 'That's a knock-out! I feel like a rag-bag beside that.'

'Just a little thing I picked up in the sales,' said Jo-Ann nonchalantly. 'Lovely to see you. Mary's in there.'

She pointed towards a closed door. The hall was empty and everything was very quiet. Charlotte moved ahead, increasingly apprehensive that she had been manoeuvred into some scheme of Jo-Ann's. So much so that she stopped in front of the door, reluctant to open it, until Jo-Ann tripped forward and flung the door wide.

The room was full of people, and the moment they saw Charlotte they started to sing, 'Happy birthday to you,' at the top of their voices.

'Surprise, surprise!' trilled Jo-Ann. 'Surprise party.' She threw her arms around Charlotte and kissed her, and these were friends who had come to Charlotte's birthday parties in past years. She was surrounded by them, overwhelmed by their kindness, as one after the other wished her happy birthday.

She wished she had dressed up. She wished she had had an inkling that this was going on. They were sorry for her this year, and this was a charity as well as a kindness. There was a buffet filling a long table, bottles in a corner bar.

'We all chipped in,' said Jo-Ann. 'They all brought bottles and the girls did the food, but I was the one who thought about it. Wasn't I?' She appealed to Mary Whitehead, the girl who ran the riding school, who said,

'Yes, you were,' as though she was still surprised about that, and looked at Charlotte and added, 'It *was* Jo-Ann's idea.'

Not what Mary would have expected from Jo-Ann, and not what Charlotte would have expected either. Charlotte said huskily, 'How kind of you all! I don't know what to say.'

She didn't understand Jo-Ann's part in this. Right from schooldays anything that Jo-Ann did usually had a selfish motive, and throwing a party for Charlotte seemed very out of character. Even if the guests were providing the food and drink.

'All my idea,' Jo-Ann repeated, and this time it was Saul she was smiling at. He stood, apart from the crush, by the wall, and a little shock ran through Charlotte as it always did when she saw him unexpectedly, like touching a live wire.

Jo-Ann left her then, to cross to Saul, and Charlotte wondered if this was intended to show him what a caring, friendly person Jo-Ann was. Whatever her reason here was a party, and here were Charlotte's friends, so Charlotte said, 'I think you're lovely, all of you. If I'd known I'd have dressed up.'

Everybody else had. Even Mary, rarely seen out of jodhpurs, was wearing a pretty floral dress, and had her short straight usually tousled hair in a sleek cap.

'As it is,' said Charlotte, 'the least I can do is let my hair down.' She was wearing a bandeau. She tugged it off and shook her head and her hair fell loose and swirling, then somebody gave her a glass of punch, and it would have been rank ingratitude not to enjoy herself after the trouble they'd taken.

A record player was providing music and Charlotte danced, and chatted and joked and flirted, and thanked everybody over and over again. Mary had made a huge quiche for the buffet, and as she cut Charlotte a slice she said, 'Well, we thought you could do with something to cheer you up, and when Jo-Ann rang me and said how

about a party and we remembered it was your birthday——'

'Thanks.' Charlotte took the plate and scooped from
various side dishes.

'But if you ask me,' said Mary, 'I think she wanted to
show off.'

'Show off what?'

'Well, everybody's been wondering if there's anything
going on between you and Saul Laurenson, although Jo-
Ann says he's been dating her.'

'That doesn't surprise me,' said Charlotte tartly.

'I think she's out to show everybody that she's got him,'
said Mary. 'They've never moved away from each other.
She's all over him, and she's never stopped smirking.'

Charlotte hadn't spoken to Saul yet. She had heard his
drawling voice through the babble of voices, but he hadn't
come over to her and she hadn't come up against him.
She would sooner or later. If she looked around she would
find him. The crowd would have to be dense that he
didn't stand out in. She tried the quiche and said, 'This is
delicious. Anyhow, he's leaving for Canada on Monday,
and he told me that half the time he can't even remember
the names of the girls he's had, so I shouldn't think Jo-
Ann's got much to grin about.'

Mary grinned, 'What a rotten thing to say! But he is
dishy, isn't he?'

Charlotte shrugged indifference, then she looked across
in the direction Mary was looking, at Saul and Jo-Ann,
and the food in her mouth turned to ashes.

They were standing, talking with others, and Jo-Ann's
hand was through Saul's arm. That was all, but searing
anger ripped Charlotte. Seeing Jo-Ann's fingers on the
stuff of Saul's coat hurt more than finding Jeremy and
Lesley naked together. She could have rushed through
the guests and physically torn them apart, and she turned

away, got herself another glass of punch and drank it quickly, thinking, I mustn't look again. So long as I don't see them I won't do anything unforgivable.

Mary had followed her and was looking at her anxiously, asking, 'Are you all right?'

'Sure,' said Charlotte. 'But I wish I'd known this was waiting. It's been a bit overwhelming.'

'Too much of a surprise?'

'A lovely surprise,' said Charlotte, then smiled at the man nearest and said, 'Shall we dance?' because that would pass the time and help get her through the lovely surprise that had turned into a nightmare.

For the next two hours she hardly stopped dancing. Anyone seeing her would have thought she was having a high old time, and she was a little high, but she knew that as soon as she stopped whirling and smiling she was going to sink into deep depression.

Saul didn't ask her to dance; he didn't come near her. When she saw him dancing with Jo-Ann she was swaying in the arms of a young man who was hoping this was his lucky night, and she leaned to whisper in her partner's ear, 'Would you do me a favour? Could you give me a lift home without breaking up the party? I had a long hard day at work and I'm dead on my feet, only I've drunk rather a lot of punch and I'm scared to drive.'

This convinced him his luck was in. But he was wrong, because all Charlotte wanted *was* a lift, and when they reached her home she thanked him and jumped out of the car, and vanished round the side of the house before he was over the shock of not being invited in.

The house was in darkness, except for a light in Nurse Betty's room, and Charlotte kept on walking. She hadn't the strength to saddle Kelly, but she knew she couldn't sleep, so she went down to the patio and across the field, through the gate over the track, then climbed up the hill to the very top. And sat down at last, under the big old chestnut tree where she had tethered Kelly that morning, long, long ago it seemed, after her first meeting with Saul.

While she was walking she was occupied. The moon was bright but the turf was uneven, she had to watch as she stepped and she walked fast, almost as though this was a race. But at the top of the hill, when she sat down, knees hunched so that her chin rested on them and hands clasped round her ankles, the thoughts came rushing into her head.

That had been a hellish party. Except for the night when she waited at the hospital, to hear if her father would live or die, she couldn't recall a night that came near it for pain. The pain was with her still, raw and aching, and nothing like the jealousy she had felt for Jeremy.

For Jeremy she had felt neither jealousy nor love, just hurt pride and makebelieve. Jeremy was something out of one of the plays he played in, but the agony of watching Saul with Jo-Ann had been real and primitive. She could have killed them. She could have picked up one of the buffet knives and stuck it into the pair of them.

If Jo-Ann had organised that party to show everybody that she had Saul Laurenson, and Charlotte hadn't, she had shown them nothing of the kind, because Saul was going in two days' time and he carried no photographs because there was never a girl he hoped to remember. But Jo-Ann had shown Charlotte, all right, what he meant to Charlotte.

Charlotte had known they were almost certainly having an affair, but *seeing* them touch had brought the terrifying realisation that she herself loved Saul, hopelessly and completely. She had recognised him that night on the patio, the moment he touched her, before he kissed her. She knew him, and it was his arms she had wanted around her. And the misery every night had nothing to do with

Jeremy. It was because Saul always walked past her door.

The day after tomorrow he would be gone. For quite a while, he'd said, and she'd thought that she couldn't imagine the house without him. But it wasn't just the house. It was her life she couldn't imagine without Saul, and she stared up at the moon, big and round and yellow as a runaway balloon, and felt like the only living soul in a world of emptiness.

She hadn't a clue what she could do. She hadn't time to do much, and even if she had how could she even start? She couldn't say, 'I love you,' because that wasn't a word in his vocabulary, and she had been saying it to Jeremy only last week. 'I love you,' instead of goodbye on the telephone, and that was all it had meant then, just, 'Cheerio.' Now it meant that she wanted to follow Saul to the ends of the earth, that she would never want another man. That she ached for him and would die for him.

She sat for a long time. She could have stayed there all night, but it wouldn't be any easier in the morning, and at last she got stiffly to her feet and began to walk back. Saul might not be home. He might have stayed at Jo-Ann's. And if he was at home, and still up, what could she say to him?

She would get a night's sleep, what was left of it, and tomorrow she would say, 'This is your last day. Let's spend your last day here together,' and she would try to make him remember her. He didn't carry photographs, but somehow she would strive to fix her image in his mind because it mattered so desperately that he should not forget her.

She was in pieces, as shaken up as though she had been caught in a hurricane and tossed to the four winds. She would crawl into bed, Georgy would be glad to see her, and lie there until morning, and perhaps by morning she would be whole.

She had a front door key on her key ring in the pocket of

her jeans, and she let herself in very quietly. Even so the dogs began barking in the kitchen. Georgy's yap was not among them, so either he was lying low or Aunt Lucy had put him in Charlotte's room before she went to bed herself.

The party at Jo-Ann's should be over by now, unless it was lasting all night. And Charlotte hoped it was lasting because, if everyone started leaving, she couldn't see Jo-Ann neglecting to offer Saul a bed for the night.

She thought, I'll go round in the morning. I left my car there. If Saul isn't back for breakfast I'll be at Jo-Ann's and I'll get him away. I'll think up something to do with the house, the business—something.

But when he strolled out of the drawing room into the hall her wits deserted her. It was light as day in here, the full moon streaming in. She could see him clear as clear, and the sight of him sent her mind reeling.

'Where have you been?' he asked and she started to chatter.

'Would you believe, sitting on top of a hill looking at the harvest moon? Or is it the hunters' moon? Which comes first, harvest or hunter? As a country girl I should surely know. Lovely party, wasn't it?'

She was backing towards the stairs, she was going to run upstairs because she couldn't face him tonight. Everything had been too much. Tonight she would just make a fool of herself.

He said, 'Charlotte,' harshly, and she froze. He looked grim as death, and she remembered that other time and whispered, 'What's happened?'

He walked back into the drawing room. The dogs had stopped barking, recognising her step and her voice. She followed him, and in here it was all grey and silver. 'What's the matter?' she was still whispering, and when Saul closed the door she sat down on the big sofa because her legs gave way.

He said, and his voice was still harsh, 'I'll tell you what's the matter. I'm in love with you and it's killing me.'

She hardly knew his face. She had never seen him anything but confident and in control. This was another man, and she held out her arms and said, 'Come here,' and he came, kneeling beside her, and she cradled his head against her breast. 'Oh, my love,' she whispered, 'my love.'

He raised his face, his lips twisted in what could have passed for a smile. 'The difficulty is,' he said, 'that I mean it. And as you keep reminding me, it's time my luck ran out. Most things have been a game up to now, and I've never been scared of losing because nothing mattered that much. The first thing in my life that really matters is getting you to marry me.'

She choked, '*Marry* you? You said you didn't want a wife.'

'I didn't.' He got up from kneeling beside her to sitting beside her, almost glaring at her. 'If I hadn't met you I never would have married. But I want you wearing my ring, and any children you have I want to be mine.'

She said, 'Oh!' and then, 'Don't tell me it was the photograph my father showed you.'

'It had nothing to do with your photograph. I took your photograph from the office at the shop and that goes wherever I go, but when we were looking around those houses and I came up into that bedroom, and you were standing there and I startled you and you stumbled against me—I don't know,' he gestured helplessly, 'I suddenly wished we'd been looking around together. Just the two of us, looking for a home. That had never happened to me before. And soon afterwards the car smash, and I could have lost you before we'd even had time to get to know each other.'

Charlotte hardly moved. She listened and thought, Yes, yes . . .

He said huskily, 'I could have torn those roses he sent you to pieces. I could have killed him when you were in his bed. And every time you spoke to him on the phone you said, "I love you," and God, how I hated him!'

'I wasn't sleeping with Jeremy that night,' she said. 'And what there was between us is over.'

'Yes.'

'Did you see him in the Stage Door?'

'I saw he saw us in the Stage Door,' said Saul with a certain satisfaction, 'which was why we were in the Stage Door. To make sure he got the message. The night I was waiting for you on the patio I'd warned him that if he didn't keep away from you I'd finish him.'

'You *didn't*! You couldn't,' she said, and she knew that he could, just as Jeremy had decided he couldn't afford to tangle with Saul.

'I'm not a naturally jealous man,' said Saul hastily, 'so don't let that worry you. If you married me I'd trust you. It's the not being sure that's hell, and not knowing what to do about it because this could be when my luck runs out. Jealousy can cut you apart. Watching you dancing tonight, then going off with some man. I've been sitting here for hours, waiting for you to come back.'

'What about Jo-Ann?' she asked. 'You've been going around with her, haven't you?'

'Would you care?' He sounded surprised and hopeful. 'As a matter of fact I haven't, although I've bumped into her more than once. And she asked me to this surprise birthday tonight.' He started to stand up. 'I've a present for you,' and she caught his hand.

'I do know what jealousy is,' she told him. 'It's seeing Jo-Ann hanging on to you and not being able to walk over and smile because you'd rather have my hand on your arm.' Her fingers tightened and Saul sat down again, cupping her face in his hands and staring into her eyes as though he would read her soul, then he said huskily,

'I'm burning up for you.'

'I know something about that too,' she said. 'I never locked my door. We could have put sleeping pills in Aunt Lucy's cocoa, anyhow she's a sound sleeper until seven o'clock in the morning.'

He smiled, his eyes as dark as the darkest night, and Charlotte said tremulously, 'I'm not joking, really. I didn't know what to do because I do love you. Not like Jeremy. Nothing like that. Nothing like anything that ever happened to me before.'

He moved away from her, but only for a moment, and put a flat jewel case on her lap, and before she opened it she knew it was the aquamarine collar. Her throat was so choked up that she could only make little cries of gratitude, and Saul closed the case again and put it down on the carpet. Then he sat beside her and took her in his arms, pressing her back into the soft cushions of the long sofa.

As he began to caress her, and desire rose in her, the words came. 'Oh, I want you to love me. I didn't know what I was going to do when you went away. I was alone on top of that hill watching the moon and wondering how I could make you remember me because——'

His mouth came down on hers, then he raised his head with a laugh that was half a groan. 'For God's sake, hold your tongue and let me love.'

'John Donne,' she cried.

'Clever girl!'

'Oh yes.' She was starving for him, her heart was beating so hard that it sounded like drums in her ears. 'I must be clever to have got you.'

'Hush,' he said, 'hush,' and for a long time their togetherness was deep and tender and savagely sublimely passionate, with no need at all of words.

Harlequin® Plus

A WORD ABOUT THE AUTHOR

As a former journalist, Jane Donnelly reported news, interviewed celebrities and reviewed television shows. But never did she even consider fiction ... until one day on a bus she overheard a girl saying to a friend: "Auntie Flo made out she didn't know he was coming, but she knew all right."

For the rest of the bus ride, Jane amused herself by imagining who "he" was and what the auntie's angle was. When she got home she wrote a little story based on the conversation and sold it. Within twelve months she was selling everything, from short thrillers to movie scripts. And then, with fifty novelettes behind her, she tried her hand at a full-length novel. The result was her first Harlequin, *A Man Apart* (Romance #1227), published in 1968.

Jane makes her home in the ancient village of Quinton, on the edge of the Cotswolds, five miles from Stratford-on-Avon—Shakespeare country. Her historic cottage was once a "witches' house," but Jane feels strongly that if any witchcraft was ever practiced there, it must have been the "white" variety—for she cannot imagine a place more filled with peace and contentment.

Legacy of
PASSION

BY CATHERINE KAY

A love story begun long ago comes full circle...

Venice, 1819: Contessa Allegra di Rienzi, young, innocent, unhappily married. She gave her love to Lord Byron—scandalous, irresistible English poet. Their brief, tempestuous affair left her with a shattered heart, a few poignant mementos—and a daughter he never knew about.

Boston, today: Allegra Brent, modern, independent, restless. She learned the secret of her great-great-great-grandmother and journeyed to Venice to find the di Rienzi heirs. There she met the handsome, cynical, blood-stirring Conte Renaldo di Rienzi, and like her ancestor before her, recklessly, hopelessly lost her heart.

Choose from this great selection of early Harlequins—books that let you escape to the wonderful world of romance!*

982 **No Orchids by Request**
Essie Summers

984 **Island in the Dawn**
Averil Ives

015 **Sweet Are the Ways**
Essie Summers

048 **High Master of Clere**
Jane Arbor

126 **Man of the Islands**
Henrietta Reid

151 **Enchanted Autumn**
Mary Whistler

156 **A Place Called Paradise**
Essie Summers

162 **Island of Love**
Belinda Dell

168 **Rose in the Bud**
Susan Barrie

172 **Let Love Abide**
Norrey Ford

173 **Red as a Rose**
Hilary Wilde

175 **Moon over Madrid**
Fiona Finlay

180 **Rose of the Desert**
Roumelia Lane

181 **Dangerous Love**
Jane Beaufort

183 **Never Call It Loving**
Majorie Lewty

1184 **The House of Oliver**
Jean S. MacLeod

1186 **Someone Else's Heart**
Barbara Allen

1187 **Sweet Adventure**
Mary Burchell

1195 **Spread Your Wings**
Ruth Clemence

1200 **Satin for the Bride**
Kate Starr

1203 **The Lucky One**
Marjorie Lewty

1204 **This Was Love**
Jean Curtis

1214 **The Marshall Family**
Mary Burchell

1215 **Soft Is the Music**
Jane Beech

1221 **Master of Melincourt**
Susan Barrie

1222 **Dark Confessor**
Elinor Davis

1237 **The Last of the Mallorys**
Kay Thorpe

1238 **White Rose of Love**
Anita Charles

1248 **Where Love Is**
Norrey Ford

1314 **Summer Island**
Jean S. MacLeod

Some of these book were originally published under different titles.

Relive a great love story...
with Harlequin Romances
Complete and mail this coupon today!

Harlequin Reader Service

In the U.S.A.
1440 South Priest Drive
Tempe, AZ 85281

In Canada
649 Ontario Street
Stratford, Ontario N5A 6W2

Please send me the following Harlequin Romance novels. I am enclosing
my check or money order for $1.50 for each novel ordered, plus 75¢ to cover
postage and handling.

☐ 982	☐ 1156	☐ 1180	☐ 1195	☐ 1221
☐ 984	☐ 1162	☐ 1181	☐ 1200	☐ 1222
☐ 1015	☐ 1168	☐ 1183	☐ 1203	☐ 1237
☐ 1048	☐ 1172	☐ 1184	☐ 1204	☐ 1238
☐ 1126	☐ 1173	☐ 1186	☐ 1214	☐ 1248
☐ 1151	☐ 1175	☐ 1187	☐ 1215	☐ 1314

Number of novels checked @ $1.50 each = $ _____

N.Y. and Ariz. residents add appropriate sales tax. $ _____

Postage and handling $ _____ .75

             TOTAL $ _____

I enclose _____
(Please send check or money order. We cannot be responsible for cash sen
  through the mail.)

Prices subject to change without notice.

NAME _____
                      (Please Print)

ADDRESS _____
                              (APT. NO.)

CITY _____

STATE/PROV. _____

ZIP/POSTAL CODE _____
Offer expires February 28, 1983.   21156000000